Karma's Here

Altered Karma Series Book 2
Jillian Beane

Jillian Beane LLC

ISBN: 979-8-9900-217-9-2 (eBook)

ISBN: 978-1-971038-01-8 (Paperback)

LCCN: 2025925461

Book Cover by Shawnna Sue & Jillian Beane

Editing by Dayna Hart at Hart to Heart Edits

1st edition 2026

Published By Jillian Beane LLC

Contents

Chapter 1

Karma

The dim light from the small lamp with a bare bulb and no shade barely penetrated the darkness of the basement to the corner where Karma sat on her cot, frustrated and angry. The light glinted off the iridescent ink embedded in her right forearm. PC in fancy scroll, the footprints of a Komodo dragon, and the number "5713" stared back at her. Karma clenched her fist, then turned and fought to stand from the cot she had lain on all night.

Ridge was already up and out of the hidey hole he called home. He'd been extremely generous, allowing her and her two teenage charges to stay with him since they couldn't return to the trailer park Karma had called home for almost two decades.

The room spun with her movement, and chills swept over her body.

If she closed her eyes to try to concentrate on steadying herself, she'd end up on her ass, so she focused on a random spot on the wall until the wave of dizziness passed, gritting her teeth so hard she thought her teeth would crack. Aches pulled at her from every joint in her body.

Karma leaned hard on the crutch, made from a branch Ridge brought back a few weeks before. He'd stripped the bark from it and smoothed it. She was forced to use it to steady herself any time she moved around.

Ridge had taken over her duties of keeping everyone safe for the last two months. When he rescued her from the Phoenix Corps facilities, after they inject-ed her with something to take away her Komodo dragon, he'd brought her back here and taken care of everything she could no longer do. He went to the trailer park and cleared out the others who lived there, helping them to find new places to inhabit. He even took some of them to the borders so that they could leave the area entirely. Ridge and Lily went out to check the traps daily for fresh meat, and the sup-ply truck they'd stolen on their way out of the facility provided canned goods and clothes to tide them over for a while. He'd kept up with Lily's training, since Karma still barely had the strength to move around their small basement even two months later. Ridge also added Peter into the mix, teaching him to fight as well.

They lay low, as much as possible. The goon squad from Phoenix Corps patrolled all around Fairway, looking for any sign that Karma and Ridge were still around, itching to recapture them after the destruction they left in their wake while escaping the clutches of the mad scientists.

Karma smiled at the memory of the explosion she and Ridge had set off on their way out of the docks. Ridge snuck up to one of the fences a few weeks ago. Phoenix Corps' loading docks were still out of commission, with scaffolding set up as they worked to rebuild the area. They hadn't even started on a new guard shack as of his last visit.

Her smile quickly dropped as she tripped over air, her leg giving out, almost dumping her into a pile on the floor. She growled in frustration.

Light flooded in from the trapdoor to their basement home, and Ridge appeared, leaping the steps and coming straight for her, wrapping his strong arm around her waist and steadying her until she got her legs back under her.

Awareness prickled over her skin as her shirt rode up, his fingers resting on the bare skin at her waist. Her breath quickened and became shallow.

His cocky grin slid over his mouth as he pulled her flush against him and dropped his forehead to hers, breathing her in. "You should be resting." His voice held a husky quality that sent shivers down her body, and his grin widened.

"I've rested for months. I need to build back my stamina, so I can at least function as a human, again."

"The fevers are less, but you are still getting them daily. Whatever they injected you with is still in your system."

She nodded, dropping her eyes. "Maybe if I can move around more, my body will get it out faster." Her voice lowered to a whisper. "I hated what they did to me, what they turned me into. But now, I can't even walk across the room to help with dinner."

Ridge lifted her, carried her over to the table, and sat down on one of the old chairs, holding her on his lap, his arms cocooning her in. "You have me now. I'm here to do what you can't, until you are back on your feet."

His thumb rubbed lazy circles on her ribs, and she struggled to have a coherent thought. "What if this never gets better?" Her voice cracked on the fear threatening to overwhelm the mix of comfort and tingles his touch caused.

"I already told you. I'm not going anywhere, Karma. I walked into hell to get you. We blew it up to get out. This? This is a cakewalk." His hand left her side and cupped her cheek. His thumb tilted her chin until their eyes met, and he dropped his lips to hers, taking her in a slow, languid kiss.

She whimpered and held tight to the security he offered, gripping the shoulders of his shirt in her fists, deepening the kiss. Memories of their one night together before Phoenix Corps had captured her engulfed her, driving her to pull him closer, wanting to climb into his skin.

Quiet laughter penetrated her senses, and she disentangled herself from him, her breathing heavy.

Lily and Peter stood at the bottom of the steps, hiding their giggles behind their hands.

Karma shifted her weight to get up, but Ridge tightened the steel bands of his arms around her, keeping her in place.

His voice had dropped another octave, and he sounded like he'd swallowed shards of glass. "Don't move yet."

She felt the evidence of his arousal against her hip as he shifted her back into him. She felt her cheeks warm.

Ridge cleared his throat. "You two get cleaned up. I'm sure you're both filthy after gardening and training."

He hadn't kissed her like that since she'd been captured by Phoenix Corps.

Ridge turned her face to him. "The bruise is finally almost gone."

She nodded. "It took much longer than it would have taken to heal even before they altered me."

"You had a lot of injuries, not to mention whatever is still fighting within you."

Karma shrugged. She bit down on her lower lip.

Ridge pulled her lip free from her teeth and kissed her again, sucking her lower lip into his mouth. His breathing had sped up again when he pulled back. "Say it."

"I'm practically useless," she said, sounding defeated even to her own ears. "Please, let me help with dinner."

"I have a map to use to get in and out of Phoenix Corps now. I'd say useless is the farthest thing from what you are."

"They could've found all of my entrances by now."

Ridge shrugged. "Maybe. But I doubt it. You were able to get in and out under their noses for *years* before they figured it out, and even then, they needed someone to tell them. For all their mad science-y smarts, they sure are morons."

Karma gritted her teeth. Karma had saved Annabeth from what Phoenix Corps did to her father. Their experiments drove him mad, and he attacked Annabeth, knocking her unconscious. When he went after her, Karma stopped him. Yet, Annabeth had gone to Phoenix Corps to get injections under Karma's nose. Then she sold her out.

Ridge dragged her into another searing kiss, drawing her back to the present. They were both breathless when he pulled away. "Forget about them. We'll deal with them when you are better. For now, let's make some dinner."

Everything in her wanted to say, "I *should have gotten better by now*." But she held her tongue and nodded.

Ridge lifted her onto her feet and kept a steadying hand on the small of her back as they walked the short distance to the kitchen. He stayed within arm's reach of her, and she caught him stealing glances at her from the corner of her eye.

Chapter 2

Ridge

Ridge followed Karma into the kitchen, distracted by her swaying hips, but keeping a close eye to make sure she was still steady on her feet. He worried constantly about her. Whatever they'd injected her with when she was in the clutches of Phoenix Corps had ravaged her system. She seemed to be taking it in stride, but she couldn't hide the fear from him.

Karma stepped up to the counter and propped the crutch he'd made her against it. Her hand trembled as she reached for a knife to chop up the herbs waiting on the countertop.

Ridge placed his hand over hers, steadying it. "I can do this."

She tightened her hand on the knife. "So can I."

He nodded and stepped to her side, grabbing his own knife to clean and prep the latest catch from their traps.

Lily and Peter emerged from the darker side of the basement and started setting up the table.

They'd turned into a little family. The thought made Ridge smile. He'd found purpose since he met them—the night he tried to steal food from Karma's traps.

Karma was as tough as they came. She'd fought fiercely for these kids, who weren't even hers.

Peter looked at Ridge as if he were a hero; it made Ridge uncomfortable. He'd done too many bad things for Phoenix Corps and was nowhere near balancing the scales with good deeds. He didn't think he ever could.

His eyes drifted back to Karma, determination written on her face as she wielded the knife. They'd had one night together. One night was all it took for his addiction to take hold. He reached out to her at every opportunity, which was rarer than he'd like, given they lived in a basement with zero privacy. Touching her brought him a peace he never thought he'd achieve.

Karma turned, a smile on her lips as well. Then the color drained from her face, and her eyes rolled back in her head.

Thankful for his lightning-fast reflexes, Ridge caught her before she hit the ground, cradling her against him as his heart pounded and silence abruptly filled the room. The kids stopped in their tracks, worry falling over their faces, replacing the rare joy they'd had for a moment.

Heat rose from Karma's skin, through her clothes, scorching his skin.

"Mud," he said, lifting her and rushing back over to the cots.

Lily and Peter scattered to grab dirt and water from the barrels they had stored.

Karma whimpered as he lay her on the stained cot.

"Shh, rest now." He stripped off her t-shirt, exposing the tank underneath and lifting it to reveal her stomach.

Her brows furrowed, and she pushed at his hands. She had very little strength, and he easily pinned her hands above her head. Prior to the injection she'd been given, he could never have restrained her so easily, even with his enhanced strength.

"We've got to cool you down, baby. Shh." He nodded for Peter to approach and pack the dirt around her torso, then to Lily, who dampened the dirt. He pulled Karma's arms back down and repeated the process over her arms, shoulders, and neck. He placed the damp rag on her forehead once all the dirt was wet.

This happened too often. They shouldn't have a routine around this. He shook his head, worry overwhelming him.

"Ridge," Lily said softly, "Peter and I will finish dinner. You stay with Karma."

Ridge managed a small smile for her. "Thanks." These kids shouldn't be faced with these hardships. They shouldn't have these responsibilities. They were just kids.

Heat radiated off her hand.

Why wasn't she getting better yet? Why was she still weaker than even a human?

Another whimper, and he pressed his lips to her scorching cheek, whispering softly, "You're safe, Karma. I won't let anything happen to you. You'll beat this. You are the strongest person I know."

He jumped away as her back bowed off the cot, disrupting the mud they'd packed around her.

Karma's head thrown back, mouth opened in a soundless scream, and her hand clutched his, tighter and stronger than it had in weeks.

A pan clattered to the floor, and out of the corner of his eye, he saw Lily gather Peter in, hiding his face.

Using his free hand, Ridge dribbled water over Karma's torso, where she'd dislodged the mudpack. Her muscles seized, not allowing him to press her back into the cot.

Fear squeezed his heart.

Slowly, her body sank back onto the cot, and tears streamed silently down her face. Ridge kissed the tear trails and rubbed circles with his thumb on the back of the hand he held, murmuring to her.

Karma remained unconscious for hours, and he refused to leave her side. Lily and Peter occupied themselves with playing cards after cleaning up the meal they prepared.

He didn't notice Lily until she placed a hand gently on his shoulder and squeezed, comforting him, as he'd done for her in the past.

"I can sit with her while you rest for a bit."

Ridge shook his head.

"You can't take care of her unless you take care of yourself."

Ridge shifted his eyes to look at her and smirked. "Using my own words against me?"

A cloud of sadness passed over her eyes. "Rosie used to say that, too. Karma needed to hear it *a lot.*"

"Rosie was a special lady. And smart," Ridge said. She'd passed away just before Karma was captured. Ridge walked over to the cot he used, pulling it next to Karma before lying down. He took her hand in his and closed his eyes.

Her hand twitching brought him out of shallow slumber. Lily and Peter were both tucked into their beds, so hours must have passed. Ridge sat up and placed his hand on her forehead.

The fever was down.

Karma blinked open her eyes. They drifted over to Ridge.

"How are you feeling?" he asked, helping to sit her up and guiding a glass of water to her lips.

Karma took a small swallow. "Like I've been run over repeatedly by one of Phoenix Corps' supply trucks." Her voice was scratchy and strained.

"This was a bad one."

Lily spoke up. "Should we try to get some kind of medicine from inside Phoenix Corps?"

"Absolutely not." "No." Ridge and Karma spoke at the same time.

"It has to work itself out of my system at some point, right?" Karma continued.

"I wouldn't even know where to start to find the right stuff to give her," Ridge chimed in. "Whatever I bring out could make things worse."

Karma gripped his hand. "I wouldn't let anything brought out of there be injected in me again. I don't care if it is labeled as a cure-all for their other concoctions." She turned her head to take in Lily. "And, you won't be going anywhere near Phoenix Corps, *ever*."

"But I can help."

"No." Their simultaneous refusal echoed off the walls of the basement.

Lily looked like she wanted to argue, but she didn't say a word. She lay back down and turned away from them.

Karma's eyes welled with tears, and she dropped her chin.

Ridge placed his fingers under her chin, bringing her eyes back to meet his. "She's worried. We all are. She wants to help."

"I hate this." Her words were barely a whisper.

Ridge lifted the damp rag from where it had fallen when she sat up and began washing away some of the mud from her neck. "I know that. You've taken care of everyone for so long. It must be hard to have to be the one taken care of."

Karma's eyes closed, and anguish spread over the features of her face.

"Hey." Ridge waited until her grey eyes opened and met his. "You *are* going to come out on the other side of this. I won't settle for anything less."

Chapter 3

Karma

Karma sat on the edge of her cot, trying to determine if she had enough energy to walk to the kitchen without falling on her face. Ridge and the kids were up on the surface. He'd said they were going to tend the garden before they left. None of them wanted to leave after her episode the evening before. But their hovering made her feel even more incompetent.

The dust drifting from the ceiling revealed someone walking on the floor above, but she couldn't hear or smell them.

She shifted her weight, preparing to move, when the trap door opened and Ridge's familiar boots stepped down the stairs. Relief flooded her.

His intense green eyes collided with hers. "You're still awake."

Karma struggled to stand before he reached her, supporting her weight with an arm around her waist.

"How are you feeling?"

She gave him the best annoyed face she could muster. "You had to help me stand up. How do you *think* I'm feeling?"

Ridge's lips pressed against her temple, then her cheek, finally landing on her lips, coaxing her to open for him, as he turned, pulling her fully against him.

Her knees went weak for an entirely different reason.

He dropped his forehead to hers and closed his eyes, breathing deeply.

"Where are the kids?" she asked.

"I've stashed them in a building about a block from the garden. I picked up a scent nearby and wanted to investigate. Turns out, the person I found wants to talk to you." He pulled back, meeting their gazes. "I don't want to take you out of here, but I also don't want him to know where we are staying."

"Who is it?" she asked.

"Jacob."

"He hasn't left?"

Ridge shook his head.

Karma stiffened, her eyes going wide. "He's not still at the trailer park, right?"

"No. I told him to leave. I'd not seen hide nor hair of him since. But he's asking to meet you there."

"What for?"

"He refused to tell me." His matter-of-fact tone failed to hide his irritation. "I don't like the idea of taking you back there."

"I need to know what he wants."

"I figured you'd say that, which is why I stashed the kids and came for you." Ridge handed her the makeshift crutch he'd made and kept his hand on the small of her back as he guided her to the stairs.

Ridge brought the kids back after making sure Jacob had left the area as he'd said he would, while Karma ate and rested for the long trek. They secured the kids in Ridge's hidey-hole with instructions to stay put. Setting out into the dim daylight, she and Ridge then worked their way toward the trailers.

Her legs felt like lead, and Ridge had been taking more and more of her weight the further they walked. Every time she tripped over air, Ridge's arms tightened around her and kept her from sprawling onto her face.

Frustration held her in a stranglehold. It was one thing to be altered. She hadn't asked for it, hadn't wanted it. But it had given her the strength and skills she needed to help others. Whatever they injected her with, it left her weaker than if they'd never altered her. She couldn't even help herself now, and it rubbed her nerves raw.

Karma got her first view of the trailer park since it had been raided. Tension and anger radiated off her, and her hands clenched into fists. She made her way to the remains of her trailer and swiped angrily at the tears spilling down her cheeks.

Her trailer had been flipped onto its side, crushing the hidden hallway she'd created and the secret cove where that herb garden had been. Any cots or remaining supplies had been carelessly tossed from the trailer and destroyed, peppering the ground with debris. Mrs. Thorn's trailer was structurally undisturbed, leaving the underground room she'd dug undiscovered.

She walked to each of the other trailers in the park to make sure no one still lived there, Ridge helping her each step.

"Judy crossed the river on the other side of Phoenix Corps, the place you told me about. Jacob said he'd make his own way. He packed up, but waited until I'd left before he headed out. His scent moved toward Phoenix Corps."

"He wouldn't go back to them." Her tone sharpened and her body stiffened.

"Didn't say that he did. That's just the direction his scent went. I left him his privacy and didn't follow it. Just checked that he'd left."

"Sorry." She laced her fingers through his. "Jacob was one of the first people I pulled out of Phoenix Corps. He kept to himself. He didn't like relying on me, or anyone, for help. I left him alone, but kept him safe. His body rejected the splicing. They tortured him, trying to override his body's immunity." Karma shook her head sadly. "I wanted to help him more."

"You helped so many."

"Not as many as Phoenix Corps hurt."

"Maybe not, but you hurt them in the process. We won't let them get away with this."

Karma didn't acknowledge his words, just turned and continued until they reached Jacob's old trailer. A chill ran down Karma's back, alarm bells ringing in her head. While her nose wasn't working, her intuition screamed at her that people hid around her, their eyes locked onto her.

She stopped walking, pulling Ridge up short when he would have moved closer.

"I won't let them harm you," he murmured out of the corner of his mouth. Ridge indicated an area to their right and ran a hand through his hair. He tilted his head and pointedly looked in three other directions. If he'd been an actual cat, his hair would've stood on end as his whole body bristled.

Karma tightened her grip on the crutch she held and pulled her weight off Ridge. He'd need to be able to move without worrying about her. She couldn't help the tightness of the expression on her face. It took all of her energy to keep herself upright; she couldn't afford to waste energy on concealing her expressions.

Jacob emerged from his trailer, his eyes locked on Karma. They trailed from her to the crutch and back again. She read the fear in his widened eyes, watched the rapid rise and fall of his chest as he panted.

Jacob had lived at the trailer park. His body rejected the splicing they'd tried to inflict on him with some type of bird, and they'd tortured him to figure out why. The result was a nearly crippled hand, the fingers gnarled and bent to the sides. His dominant hand's wrist was permanently fused at an odd and unusable angle. He stayed at the trailer park, but he didn't like anyone else who lived there.

Karma glanced at Ridge. His posture oozed aggression, and his claws, unsheathed, glinted in the dim light that reached the ground.

"Ridge said you needed to talk to me?"

Jacob stared at her with hostility. He didn't speak.

"We're not going to hurt you, Jacob." Karma softened her tone, hoping to put him at ease.

His eyes flicked to Ridge and back.

She didn't think Ridge could look any larger or intimidating than he already did, but somehow, he bristled even further. Getting the conversation moving as quickly as possible would be the safest for everyone, so she poked the bear in the way she knew was guaranteed to elicit a response. "Jake." Pip had called him that; it triggered him the same way it did when anyone called her 'pet.'

"Jacob!" he roared.

Ridge shifted in front of her in the blink of an eye, her own personal shield.

Karma patted Ridge's shoulder and stepped to the side, leaning heavily on her crutch. He didn't stop her.

"Well, we've got one word. Let's see if we can build on that."

Jacob bared his teeth.

Ridge bristled, but Karma squeezed his hand.

"Why didn't you leave Fairway after leaving the trailer park? Why didn't you go across the river?"

He glared at her.

"I only want to help you, Jacob. That's all I've wanted since I pulled you out of Phoenix Corps so many years ago."

"You should've left me there. At least then, I might be dead instead of like *this!*"

"You've hated me since I pulled you out. This is why?"

His voice dropped to a whisper. "You should have left me there."

"I told you when I pulled you out. No one deserves the fate Phoenix Corps intended for any of us caught there."

Jacob scoffed at her. He'd never been overly friendly or even mildly trusting.

Movement alerted her that there were others. Ridge swung his gaze to the side and shifted her position, putting himself between her and a bigger threat.

A large man with a slightly hunched posture stared with a hard scowl, his teeth bared, his massive chest puffed out at the corner of Judy's old trailer.

Karma turned her back to Ridge, taking in a woman nearly as big as the man emerging from Annabeth's trailer.

They'd been boxed in.

Chapter 4

7619

Ridge

They were in the open. This section of the trailer park had nothing but other trailers, five to be exact, and each one had a new occupant. He couldn't shield Karma from all sides. He'd brought her here, and now he couldn't protect her.

Ridge faced the largest man, viewing him as the most immediate threat, but that put the heavily muscled woman, nearly the same height as the man, directly at his back.

He shifted his weight and extended his clawed hands in each of their directions. It put Jacob directly behind him, in front of Karma.

Jacob was a thin whip of a man, with gnarled hands. With her crutch, Karma should be able to handle him if needed.

That left the smaller woman with a pixie cut of dark hair at his front, and an unknown man between the two women, who kept hidden in the shadows of the last trailer.

Ridge loosened his posture and unfocused his eyes, tracking their movements in his periphery.

The large man picked up a hunk of rock or concrete from the ground, tossing it absently, while his eyes bored into Ridge. The woman swung a piece of re-bar, twirling it like a majorette, and whistled a happy tune.

The unknown man peeked his head around the doorframe, not venturing into the light himself, but gesturing wildly to the others with his hands. "You don't belong here, cat." The deep bass of the voice reverberated in the air. Surprisingly, that voice did not come out of the large man to Ridge's right; it came out of the scrawny man who kept himself hidden.

"I'll be on my way soon."

"You'll be on your way now."

The big man cracked his knuckles and rolled his shoulders.

"When Karma's ready, we will leave."

"She's not leaving." The voice of the woman with the rebar rivaled the depth of the hidden man.

Ridge laughed without humor. "I'd like to see you try to stop us."

The twirling of the rebar abruptly stopped, and the woman tucked it against her body, violence oozing from her every pore.

Karma pressed her back into his. Not only could she *not* fight, but while fighting, he'd need to keep her safe.

Ridge ground his teeth together as scenarios, all of them ending poorly, swirled in his head.

The two largest people took one step, then another. The man's fists clenched.

Karma widened her stance, and he took more of her weight. A quick glance showed him that she held her crutch like a staff in a defensive posture, ready to block or strike.

His split attention caused him to miss the man's movement. The hunk of concrete collided with his temple, and he saw stars. Ridge struck out at the woman, who'd taken advantage of him being stunned, and closed the distance. He blocked her swing of the rebar, wrenching it from her grasp and shoving her hard into the large man closing the distance between them.

A shrill whistle penetrated the air. Ridge ignored the pain in his head and the ringing in his ears. He glanced around to see the two assailants on their knees.

The scrawny man who'd stayed hidden in the trailer emerged, holding his fingers to his mouth as the sound shrilled on.

Karma lifted the piece of concrete that had smashed into Ridge's head. "Cut that shit out!" Karma shouted, tossing it in the whistler's direction. It dropped to the ground a few feet in front of him and skidded across the ground, stopping when it hit the toe of the man's boot.

The whistling abruptly cut off.

Ridge struggled to his feet. Dizziness washed over him. He reached out a steadying hand and laid it on the small of Karma's back.

Had he not had the physical contact with her, he'd have missed the slight sway that indicated she was weakening again. This was too much for her in her current state.

The man and woman stumbled to their feet, shaking their heads to clear the ringing they must've been feeling too, and backed away at a hand gesture from the whistler. Ridge kept them in view, while Karma had laser focus on the man in front of her.

"Attacking him isn't a good way to get my attention." Karma's voice held a lethal edge to it.

"We've been looking for you." The whistler had a melodic lilt in his tone.

"You've got me here. You might regret that." Karma waved her free arm around, indicating the trailer park around them. "After this."

"We don't *need* him."

"Package deal. And hurting him? That's only going to leave you a few minions short. And zero help from me."

The whistler acknowledged her with a nod. He made a gesture with his hand, and the others backed up a few more paces, but the big man snarled at Karma.

Ridge adjusted his stance, ready to defend her if the man so much as twitched in her direction.

Karma pointed her crutch at him, more of her weight leaning on Ridge. "Had you not fallen to your knees when 'Boss Man' over there whistled, you'd still be picking up your teeth. Don't tempt me."

Big man clacked his teeth together, biting the air at her. Only Karma's hand on his wrist kept Ridge from closing the distance and making him regret the move.

The whistler made another, sharper motion with his hand, and the big guy backed down.

Karma reached back and clutched Ridge's hand. The tremor in her hand illustrated just how close she was to collapse. The end of the crutch rested back on the ground, and her other hand had a white-knuckled grip on it.

"What exactly is it that you want from me?" she asked.

"Not here." The waif of a man turned on his heel and headed toward the trailer park boundary.

Karma didn't move.

Ridge stayed at her side.

A minute later, his bony shoulders reappeared. "Coming?"

Karma kept her feet planted. "Where? Why?"

"Look," he started, annoyance evident in his tone.

"No. You *look*." Karma pointed the crutch at him, and Ridge snaked his arm around her waist to hold her upright. "You surrounded us and attacked. I don't know you from Adam. I certainly don't trust you. You want me to blindly follow you? Fat chance."

"You think you have a choice in the matter?"

His minions readied for another fight.

Karma huffed. "You can try them again. I don't like your odds. But it's your bet to take."

Ridge really hoped her bluff worked. Blood ran down his face from where the hunk of concrete had connected, and Karma wasn't in any shape to help.

The scrawny guy waved off his minions. "Then where?"

"You used Jacob to lure us. I'm sure he won't mind hosting."

Chapter 5

Karma

Without waiting for a response, she turned and shouldered her way into Jacob's home, pulling Ridge behind her. Karma hid her exhaustion and weakness, unwilling to give these people any upper hand. The crutch and Ridge were the only things keeping her on her feet. The tremors grew harder and harder to hide.

Once inside, she grabbed a rag from the kitchen counter, sat Ridge on the built-in bench, and proceeded to clean up the blood from his face, ignoring Jacob's sulking and the others entering the small room.

Karma took her time cleaning the blood on his face and checking for other injuries, ignoring the others but keenly aware of their every movement.

"I'll live," he said, taking the rag from her hand and setting it on the table. Ridge closed his fingers around hers. He turned blazing neon green eyes on the others. "What exactly do you want from us?"

Jacob held up his hands in surrender when Ridge's eyes landed on him.

"The *cat* was not part of the agreement," the leader pouted.

"Next time, don't ambush Karma, and *the cat* won't have to get involved."

Jacob addressed Karma. "That's Malcolm. He used to work at Phoenix Corps as one of their pencil pushers or something. He says he doesn't like them any more than we do. There are some records inside he stashed."

"Let me guess. He wants us to go in and get them out."

Malcolm interrupted. "There's no 'us' here. I want *you* to go in, Karma. I never agreed to have the cat involved." Malcolm shoved off the wall he leaned on and tried to appear intimidating. It failed miserably.

Karma raised her eyes, keeping her hand tightly on Ridge. "He has a name. It's Ridge. Use it. He's not a cat."

"And I told you outside," Ridge began, irritation riding every word. "We're a package deal."

Malcolm stepped forward again, unsuccessfully attempting to pressure them.

Karma gave a humorless laugh. "You've taken the wrong tactic if you think that you can intimidate either of us."

"Look," Malcom took a deep breath. "Jacob filled me in on the things you've done to make life difficult for Phoenix Corps. I want to get my papers out of there. It has records of the experiments from this facility, notes about their practices, and information about the earthquake." Malcolm pointed at the petite woman with the pixie cut. "That's Allie. She is very adept at blowing shit up when needed."

Malcolm introduced Duke, the large man who'd thrown the concrete at Ridge's head, and Meg, the muscular woman with the deep voice.

Karma shot Jacob a side-eye and clenched her jaw. "Where the hell did you find these people, Jacob? And why are you hanging around with them?"

Jacob's eyes dropped. His lips moved, but she didn't hear what he said.

Ridge's quick intake of breath told her he'd heard. "You went to Finley Avenue?" Ridge asked sharply.

The hair on her arms stood on end at the mention of Finley Avenue. She'd only been through that area a handful of times, and she stayed on the outskirts when she had to go near it. Gangs ruled the territory of Finley Avenue before the quake. Drug deals, murders, organized crime, and rival gangs made the area a war zone. There wasn't a night when an incident in the area of Finley Avenue didn't make the news.

During the initial quake, when chaos reigned everywhere else, the crime lords rose up and locked down the area, keeping outsiders away from their resources, hoarding food and weapons.

As the aftershocks continued, a tank holding chemicals from one of the manufacturing facilities in the area ruptured, spewing toxic liquid and gases into the air. Before the total collapse of the communication networks, there were reports that the chemicals had turned the entire area into a toxic death zone. Between the fear of the known violence and the rumor of the toxicity, no one, not even Phoenix Corps, went to the area.

Jacob's eyes landed on Allie, then drifted back over to Ridge. "I wouldn't survive out of Fairway on my own." He held out his hands. "He said I had to leave the trailer park. I didn't know where else to go."

Ridge addressed Malcolm. "Did Jacob bother to mention why it was *me* telling him to move out of the trailer park and not Karma?"

Malcolm shook his head.

Karma eyed the man and woman who'd attacked outside and laid her hand on Ridge when he made a move to stand, putting himself between her and the others. "They caught me and injected me with something to try to undo my DNA splicing. I've been sick since. It worked. I've been weaker than an un-altered human for *months*."

His eyes got big, and Malcolm stood up again. "But... out there..." he stuttered.

Karma tapped her crutch on the floor. "This and Ridge were the only things keeping me on my feet. I don't know how you'd expect me to sneak into Phoenix Corps. It's all I can do to walk a couple of blocks, and that is *with* help."

"Did no one ever tell you that you shouldn't alienate someone you want to help you?" Ridge asked. "Attacking either of us is not the way to get us to do a damn thing for you."

Malcolm shifted uncomfortably. "We weren't trying to attack Karma."

Karma crooked her finger at him, beckoning him closer.

When he was in reach, she summoned every ounce of energy she possessed. Karma shoved the crutch between his knees and twisted. The bottom half hit the back of one knee, while the top half crisscrossed just above his other knee. She shoved with all her might against the top half, knocking him off balance, his arms waving in the air as he tried to right himself.

Malcolm landed on the floor on his ass.

"I'm in no condition to help you. Even if I was, you went about this the wrong way."

Ridge lifted her into his arms and backed out of the trailer, keeping the others in sight. "You follow us, and you won't survive the night."

The last thing she saw was Jacob putting himself in the doorway, blocking the others from following them, as Malcolm screamed and ranted.

Chapter 6

Karma

Three days later, Karma sat at the kitchen table, playing solitaire, while Ridge and the kids tended to the garden and trained. Her fevers over the last few days had drained her of what little energy she had, and her frustration continued to build.

The sound of screeching tires had Karma on her feet, clutching her crutch and moving toward the trap door.

She was out of breath by the time she positioned herself behind the stairs of the trap door. Karma cursed her weakness and tried to steady her breath, as heavy footsteps pounded over the floor above her. She gripped her crutch like a baseball bat.

Angry voices reached her, muffled through the floor, too much for her to make out the words.

Karma adjusted her grip.

What sounded like bricks shattering, with shrapnel raining down on the floor, had her staring hard at the trapdoor, waiting for any movement.

Metal clinked and bonged as more debris was thrown or hit. Each sound ratcheted her anxiety.

A loud crack from inside the room stopped all movement above her. She held her breath, listening and waiting. More thunderous footsteps continued a few moments later, and additional voices joined the shouts from before.

What seemed like an eternity later, the footsteps finally receded, and she heard the vehicle drive away. Karma sank to her knees and dropped the pieces of her crutch in her lap. It was splintered where she'd grasped it too tight and twisted.

The adrenaline dump was fading. Her hands shook, and she'd become lightheaded. She bent forward, putting her head against the cool, cracked, concrete floor.

She couldn't stop a quiet moan when footsteps once again sounded above her. Her limbs felt like thousand-pound jelly noodles. She tightened her hand around the largest remaining piece of the crutch, but didn't bother to try to move. If they came into the basement, she might have one good swing left in her, if she didn't move until they were close enough to hit.

Shivers ran down her spine as the trap door was thrown open and the steps were taken in a single leap.

"Karma!" Ridge's panicked voice was music to her ears.

"Here," she called out softly.

Ridge spun and closed the distance between them, gathering her into his arms. His hands roamed over her, searching for any sign of injury. "Are you hurt? Did they come in here?"

She shook her head no, but couldn't stop trembling. "The kids?"

"We weren't nearby when I heard the truck. I have Lily and Peter stashed away. I wasn't sure what I'd find here." He pressed his lips to the crown of her head and pulled her more fully against him. "They trashed what was left upstairs. It's only because they share one brain cell among them that they didn't find the door."

"We need to move." Karma's dejected tone hit him straight in the heart. She shifted out of his reach.

Only then did he notice the pieces of the crutch on the ground. Ridge ground his teeth together. "I thought you said they didn't come down here." He pointed at the broken pieces of the crutch.

"They didn't," she said defensively. "I was waiting behind the stairs, ready to use the crutch as a weapon. I gripped it too hard."

She shrugged and moved away, struggling to get to her feet.

"Just the adrenaline," she answered his unspoken question.

Ridge reached forward, taking most of her weight and helping her to her unsteady feet. "Rest while I get the kids. I have an idea of another place we can go for a bit, but it'll be a haul to walk there. Much further than the trailer park."

Karma's legs wobbled beneath her as their makeshift parade slunk from building to building.

Ridge listened for any sounds at the front, monitoring scents before waving them across roads and down alleys.

They trudged through a neighborhood Karma hadn't visited for years. It was much further from Phoenix Corps than her trailer park had been and closer to the epicenter of the damage from the quake ten years before. Most of the buildings were completely flattened, leaving piles of debris, splintered wood, every size of brick from whole to sand, shards of steel beams and rebar, sheared-off pipes, and nests of wires interspersed through the piles.

As Ridge ushered the kids into yet another alley, he stayed behind, his hand on the small of her back, supporting her and guiding her across the rippled and cracked pavement of the once four-lane road. "Doing okay?"

Karma nodded. "Tired, but I'm ok." She leaned heavily on the new branch he'd brought her. This one wasn't as smooth as the last, but it did its job and helped her to keep going.

"We're nearly there. Just another block or so."

Ridge's arms were laden with boxes of supplies, and he had a makeshift pack strapped to his back with other supplies. Lily and Peter also carried boxes, though Karma would bet money that their boxes were *much* lighter than his. She tried unsuccessfully to tamp down her increasing frustration.

They made their way down one alley and halfway down the next when Ridge stopped and pushed them back into a hidden cove. He dropped his burdens at their feet and held a finger to his lips. He slipped back out of the cove and disappeared out of sight for what felt like endless minutes.

Lily turned to her, opening her mouth to say something, but quickly closing it again at the shake of Karma's head.

The longer Ridge was gone, the closer Peter scooted to Karma, until he was pressed into her side. Karma placed a reassuring hand on his shoulder and tried to tamp down her own anxiety. Shadows were deepening as the sun lowered in the sky and the winds picked up, carrying the scent of rain in the air, but still they waited.

It felt like an eternity later, a light drizzle slowly coating them, when Ridge finally returned. Peter rushed to his side, tucking in close, as Ridge ruffled his hair.

"This way." Ridge canted his head to the side as he picked his boxes up and backed out of the cove, Peter tight to his heels.

Lily hung back with Karma. "Do you know where he's taking us?"

Karma shook her head.

Ridge turned to look over his shoulder. "This is where I made my escape from Phoenix Corps. The last job I went on for them."

The badger's house. He'd only talked about it once, but she remembered. The man had kids, and instead of capturing him, Ridge had helped to get the badger and his family out of Fairway.

They crossed what must have once been a quaint little side street into a leveled neighborhood. Half of a couple of chimneys were still standing, but nothing else stood. There was no evidence that any effort had been made to clean up the area. It looked like the buildings had fallen, and the people had just up and left.

Hunks of light blue-green siding peeked out of the pile they were walking toward. They walked between that pile and another into what would have been the backyard. A gigantic branch from a large tree in the neighbor's yard nearly obscured the bulkhead doors leading to a stairway to a basement.

Ridge set his boxes in the grassy area and heaved, lifting the door and the branch in a single movement. The metal groaned, and with the door open, she could now tell that the hunk of branch was attached to the door.

He turned, scooping Karma into his arms, and led the way down the stairs, calling back, "Watch your heads." He tightened his arms around her as she tried to wiggle free. "You've walked enough for to-day," he growled in her ear.

Ridge kept her tight against him, releasing her with one arm to turn the knob on the door at the bottom of the stairs.

The basement opened up in front of her. A small kitchen was tucked into one side, along with some furniture which must have been on the other floors of the house at one time, and looked to be in pretty good condition. He set her down on the cushy-look-ing couch in the center of the largest area of the room, and it was comfortable too. There were two wingback chairs completing the small sitting room, and several doors in the room as well.

Karma sank into the soft fabric and intact padding of the couch. Lily and Peter's quiet, excited voices reached her as they set down their boxes and ex-plored the new space.

The thud of the bulkhead door closing brought her attention back to Ridge, carrying in his heavy boxes.

He dropped them on the floor and made his way to the couch, sinking beside her and pulling her close.

Karma snuggled in, wishing her dampened clothes would dry faster. She smiled as he tightened his arm around her and nuzzled just below her ear. He didn't lift his head to look, only pointed to the door nearest the kitchen area when Lily asked where the bathroom was. She felt his smile spread against her skin as Lily marveled at the bathroom behind the door.

Peter bounced into one of the wingback chairs. "Why were you living in the other basement, if you had access to this?" He spread his arms out, indicating the surprisingly nice area they now occupied.

Ridge picked his head up, looking at Peter, but kept Karma pressed tightly to him. "You saw how long that walk was. It's longer when you have to backtrack and detour to avoid someone being able to follow your scent. It wasn't practical."

Bouncing back up, Peter darted to one of the doors on the same wall as the bathroom. "What's in here?"

Ridge motioned with his hand to go ahead and waited.

Peter came out of the room with a big smile and eyes wide. "There's a *real* bed in there! Bunk beds!"

"The badger was resourceful. He scavenged a lot of good stuff, and he got to a lot of it before the weather or looters could."

"There's a real bed in here, too!" Lily exclaimed from the other door on that side.

"I'd better get back for another load of supplies. Do you want to go lie on a real bed, or stay here on the couch for a bit?" Ridge asked. His voice had the husky quality to it that sent shivers to her toes.

"We have food for tonight. Stay. Don't go back out there tonight."

"We should get everything moved here as quickly as we can. With them sniffing around right above my place, it's only a matter of time."

"Please stay." Karma's words were quiet. She lifted her eyes shyly to him and gripped his hand. An irrational fear was riding her hard, and she couldn't shake the feeling that he needed to stay here.

He must have read something in her eyes because he pulled her legs over his and tucked her closer to his body, cradling her.

Chapter 7

Ridge

Karma's breathing grew even as the kids explored their new home, then sat down to play cards. Ridge was content to hold Karma while she slept. He really should get up and head back to bring back their other supplies from the hidey hole he'd used as his home the last several years, but he didn't want to leave her and the kids any more than she wanted him to leave.

He was happy to find that her skin was still cool to the touch when he lifted her and carried her to the door on the opposite side from where Lily and Peter had found and claimed their bedrooms. He opened the door, careful not to disturb her sleep, and entered the dimly lit room.

A real bed waited for them in there, too. Edmund had done a great job of making this basement a real home for him and his kids. If they only paid attention to the basement, it resembled a house from before the quake, all the comforts from before. This room had a small fireplace tucked into the exterior wall and smooth wood planks covering the concrete floor beneath. They wouldn't be able to use the fireplace, since it would quickly give away their location, but the ambiance was still nice. The walls were painted light grey, and a forest of trees covered the headboard wall in a beautiful mural.

Ridge lay Karma on the soft mattress, brushing her hair out of her face, his touch lingering on her cheek, and quietly tiptoed out of the room.

Lily stood in the kitchen, prepping food, when he emerged.

"How is she?" Lily asked, worry clouding her eyes.

"No fever so far."

She gave a small smile and returned to her preparations.

"Can I come with you to get more supplies?" Peter asked.

Ridge placed his hand on Peter's shoulder. "I plan to take you with me to help gather the stuff from the garden so we can transplant it. Lily, I'd like your help with gathering some of the traps, too."

Lily nodded. "Will Karma stay here? That walk took a lot out of her."

"Yes." He knew the kids worried. They'd only known Karma as Altered. She'd always been stronger, tougher, and full of energy. This Karma... they were scared.

The next morning, after a thankfully fever-free night, Ridge set Karma up on the couch while he and the kids headed back to the trailer park, garden, and his place to gather what they could carry to bring to their new home. He was careful in the routes they took, squirreling around more than they had the day before. Getting Karma to the new house quickly was the priority before. Now, masking their scent paths and scoping out the neighborhood took precedence.

They made it to the garden first, so he set Lily and Peter to the task of dismantling it for transport to a new location. Ridge planned to leave some of the plants behind for others.

Ridge moved on to his place, but stopped short of it. Several building skeletons stood between him and the hidey hole, but he hesitated to approach. There had been a lot of activity in this area recently. A lot. He could make out the scents of at least half a dozen other Altereds from Phoenix Corps.

He crept behind partial walls as he made his way toward the place he'd called home. Approaching his building from the side with the most cover, he peered through a hole in one of the brick walls of the building next door.

The trap door stood open, and the cots they'd used were bent at odd angles, the mattresses shredded to ribbons. A fist-sized hole was punched into two of the barrels. A third barrel was crushed.

The scents were old, like the scents down the block, so they were long gone, but Ridge wasn't taking any chances. He turned on his heel and met up with the kids where he'd left them. They had the majority of the garden dismantled and ready to go.

"Where's the supplies?" Lily asked, gently placing some sage into the box.

"It's a good thing we left when we did," was all he could say. "I'll collect some of the supplies from one of the buildings down the other street that I used for overflow. We'll wind our way back and pick up the traps along the way."

Peter looked around nervously.

"They're gone for now. Let's finish up and work our way back home." Ridge's back tensed as he scanned the area. He didn't want to alarm the kids, but they needed to move quickly. The goon squad would be back.

They skirted past the trailer park. Ridge zipped around the area, pulling the traps, and carried them back to where he'd stashed the kids before entering the compound. They needed to get back to Karma.

Lily carried the traps, while Ridge toted the large box from the garden. Peter carried their meager catch from the few traps they'd gotten lucky with. They weaved their way around blocks, through alleys, and backtracked through several neighborhoods before finally getting to the neighborhood they would be calling home. Lily helped him set traps in some of the neighboring areas far enough away from their new home to keep their location a secret.

Ridge led them to Edmund's garden. It was still producing some herbs from the original planting, but weeds had choked out a lot of it. They spent the next hour in silence, weeding and replanting the garden, then made their way to their new home.

Karma stood near the sink, slicing some of the meat from their last catch and some herbs.

Peter bounded over to her, wrapping his arms around her, then presenting her with a bunch of dandelions he'd picked on their travels.

"Thanks, buddy!" Karma praised and lifted her eyes to his over Peter's shoulder. The smile she wore faded with whatever she read there. "What happened?"

"Nothing. Everyone is safe."

"Something is wrong."

Lily took the knife from Karma's trembling hand, and Ridge guided her to the cushy sofa.

"Phoenix Corps was at my place last night." At her frightened look, he added, "They were long gone by the time I got there, but they trashed the place. Destroyed what little supplies were left there. It was just like the damage at the trailer park."

"I'm glad you didn't go back last night."

"How are you feeling today?" he asked, changing the subject.

"A mild fever shortly after you left, but other than that, no changes to report."

He dropped a chaste kiss on her forehead and gathered her close. She'd felt like she would break when he held her since he brought her home from Phoenix Corps. He tried to stifle the smile tugging at his lips as she melted into his embrace. Little by little, over the last couple of days, she was stronger. A week ago, she'd never have made the long hike to this neighborhood. Her body wouldn't have allowed it. Yes, it took a lot out of her, but she did make it.

His body stirred, as it usually did when she was in his arms, and he gritted his teeth. They hadn't talked about the night they spent together. All of Ridge's energy was spent making sure she and the kids were safe and cared for. Terror gripped him, afraid he would mess up, that he wasn't good enough or capable enough to take care of them. He'd been on his own for so long and had only to care for himself. He couldn't let his mind go to the possibility that Karma wouldn't recover from whatever they injected her with.

Karma placed her hand on his thigh and turned her face to his. He tried to ignore the heat in her eyes.

"What's wrong?" she asked, squeezing his thigh with her slender fingers.

The dark circles around her eyes were more due to her body's struggle against the serum they'd injected her with, and less because of the black eye Pip had given her. But her skin was paler than it had been, and her cheeks were more sunken than he remembered.

Ridge lifted a hand to her cheek, his thumb grazing back and forth over the skin. "How are you really feeling?"

She closed her eyes and leaned into his touch. "I'm tired. I'm tired of being sick, tired of letting you and the kids do everything."

"You'll get past this. It is just going to take some time."

"Too much time."

"I can see how it feels that way."

Karma's eyes drifted to where the kids stood. Her voice lowered to a whisper only he could hear. "What if it never gets better? If I'm weaker now than I was before I was altered, how will I keep them safe?"

Ridge pulled her gaze back to him. "I'm not going anywhere, Karma. I wasn't planning on abandoning you before this. I'm certainly not going anywhere now." He pressed her head against his shoulder. "Rest, baby."

Karma's hand fisted his worn, black t-shirt, but she didn't fight him; she just sank against him, and her whole being relaxed into him.

A bit later, he roused Karma enough to get her to eat, and they sat wrapped together on the couch, watching Lily and Peter play a lively game of cards at the table, once dinner was cleaned up. He was content to hold her right now, reassuring himself that her skin was still cool to the touch, that she was here with him and safe.

Lily and Peter headed to their rooms a little after Karma's breathing had evened out again, indicating she had fallen back to sleep.

Careful not to disturb her, Ridge carried her back to her new room. He placed her on the bed and pressed a kiss to her temple. He backed away to go back to the couch, but Karma grabbed his arm before he was out of reach.

"Stay."

Chapter 8

Karma

Ridge paused when she spoke.

She tightened her fingers around his wrist, just below his Phoenix Corps tattoo, and tugged.

He backed up a step and sat on the edge of the bed. Ridge reached out with his other hand and brushed a stray lock of hair out of her face and behind her ear, sending tingles down her spine.

Karma pulled him to her, sealing her mouth to his, unable to stop the sigh as his strong arm traveled behind her, closing the distance between their bodies. Her heartbeat raced and her breathing quickened.

His tongue glided over hers as he twisted his body, lying beside her and pulling her flush against him. Ridge's hand snaked down, skimming across the skin peeking between the hem of her shirt and the waistband of her pants. She trembled at the contact, and he pulled away, his own ragged breathing matching hers.

"You should rest." His voice sounded like he'd swallowed glass, rough and deep.

"I'm tired of resting." Using more strength than she thought she had, Karma yanked at Ridge, pulling him back down to her.

The length of him was hard against her belly, and she arched up and tightened her arms around him, pulling him ever closer.

Karma pulled at the hem of his shirt, rewarded when he pulled away just enough to allow her to remove it completely. Her shirt followed close behind. A sigh left her lips as his bare skin caressed hers.

It had only taken their one time together for her to be addicted to the feel of him, the connection with him.

Ridge's lips crashed back into hers, demanding submission, and she gave in, opening to him and tightening her arms around him.

Lost in his kiss, Karma's hands roamed his back and chest, reveling in the softness and steel of his skin and muscles. The ripple of the muscles beneath her touch was proof that he was just as affected by her as she was by him.

Snaking her hand between them, she reached for the button on his jeans, only to be halted when his hand closed over hers.

Ridge dropped his forehead to hers, breathing heavily. His head shook slightly side to side. "We should stop. Wait until you are better."

Karma shifted her hand, caressing him over his jeans. "It's been months. I may never get better. I need you now." She didn't hide the pleading in her voice.

Pain crossed his features, and his eyes closed. He was going to refuse her.

She stroked him again, then removed her hand, turning it and linking their fingers together.

Ridge brought their joined hands up and kissed the knuckles on hers. His hardness pressed against her, making her squirm. He lowered his mouth to hers, the kiss slow and languid. The reverence he conveyed with it brought tears to her eyes. His lips left hers, nipping at her chin and neck, working his way down her body, removing their remaining clothes as he went.

Karma writhed beneath him. She whimpered when he returned to her mouth, his tongue sweeping inside as he slid home. Tears leaked from her eyes.

He abruptly stopped moving, taking all of his weight off her and brushing at the tears. Concern laced his voice. "Am I hurting you?"

She couldn't speak over the lump in her throat, the words of love sticking there. Shaking her head, she pulled him back down, urging him to move with her legs and sealing their mouths again.

Stars exploded behind her eyes as her climax crashed over her, her arms tightening around him. He swallowed her cries as he followed her over.

She lay, wrapped in Ridge's arms, sweat cooling on her body. Karma's mind wandered as she absently traced the "7619" on his tattoo, just below the scripty PC and the panther prints.

"What are you thinking so hard about in there?" Ridge tapped her softly on the temple.

"I just…"

When she didn't continue, Ridge shifted and turned her onto her back, looking down at her face. "Talk to me," he pleaded.

Karma steadied herself with a deep breath. "How do I go forward from here? I no longer have the ability to protect the kids, to hunt and trap, and bring home food and supplies for them." She closed her eyes against the pain welling up in her core at the thoughts threatening to overwhelm her.

"Hey." Ridge waited until she opened her eyes and looked at him before speaking again. " It's skill, not brawn, that allowed you to hunt and trap. As for protecting—yes, you don't have the strength you had before, but you still have those skills, too. If you didn't believe on some level that someone who isn't altered could learn to protect themselves, you would never have started teaching Lily and Peter." Ridge placed a finger over her lips to silence the protest she was about to utter. "And yes, against an Altered, Lily had trouble defending herself; her lack of enhanced strength was a disadvantage. However, there are many people in the world who haven't been altered, and even they can pose a threat. You gave her a great start on her training. I'm adding to it. And *when* you are well enough, I expect you to take over and teach her more."

Karma steeled herself for the next thing she would say. She closed her eyes against the intensity of his neon green eyes on her. She felt like she was shouting to get it out before she changed her mind, but only heard her voice in a whisper. "And when you go, what will we do then?"

Ridge placed a kiss on each of her eyelids and stared down at her without speaking.

She could feel his eyes on her, intense and nerve-wracking.

"I walked into hell for you, and we set it ablaze on our way out. Baby, you are stuck with me."

Chapter 9

Karma

Karma stretched and curled into the warmth that was Ridge, a smile spreading across her face.

His arms tightened around her, and his voice growled into her ear. "It's still early. Rest."

"I'm feeling pretty good right now."

He pressed his lips to her temple. "No fever this morning."

"Or last night."

His smile mirrored hers. "Good."

Karma dressed and headed out to prepare break-fast. Lily and Peter hadn't come out of their rooms yet. Aches in most of her joints still plagued her, but in general, she was stronger today than she had been since her last visit to Phoenix Corps.

After breakfast, Ridge and Peter went to check on the garden, and Lily stayed with Karma. As they sat on the couch, Karma sipped her dandelion "coffee" and Lily worked on her weaving. They discussed where Lily and Ridge had placed the traps around the new neighborhood.

"Ridge said there might be some squirrels and rab-bits this far out of the main city. Do you think?"

Karma's mouth watered at the idea they'd have something other than rat meat. "I hope so. The herbs help, but I'll be grateful for something differ-ent for a change."

Lily was quiet for a while, concentrating on her weaving and adjusting her stitch to create the sides of the basket she was working on. "What's outside?"

Karma moved to the edge of the couch, alert. "What do you hear?"

Lily's hand on Karma's forearm pressed her back. "I don't hear anything. Sorry to scare you. I was just wondering..." her voice trailed off.

"What's outside? Like outside of Fairway?"

"Yeah."

"Honestly, I don't know." Karma tucked her legs back underneath her and relaxed into the fluffy cushions of the couch. "Before the quake happened, I was too poor to go anywhere. Fairway was all I knew. After… well, after the quake, chaos reigned and communication collapsed.

"I don't know how widespread the damage is. Is everywhere like it is here? I couldn't leave. What if Dorian came back? Then, I went to Phoenix Corps for help, and I couldn't leave."

"But after you escaped?"

"I found Mrs. Thorn again. By that time, she was really sick. Too sick to survive a journey that would take days at least, weeks or months most likely. And to find what? It could be worse out there, and we wouldn't know until it was too late. And I couldn't let Phoenix Corps keep doing what they were doing without any consequence or recourse. I wanted to destroy them.

"By the time Mrs. Thorn passed, you and Peter were with me."

"We held you back." The sadness in Lily's tone and words stole Karma's breath.

Karma grabbed Lily's hands, pulling them away from her weaving. "No, that's not what happened." She took a deep breath and steadied herself. "Every single one of the reasons I just gave you is true. But none of them is the thing that held me back. Fear held me back. I was afraid. I still *am* afraid."

Lily gathered her in her arms, and tears sprang to Karma's eyes. "If you want to try, we'll go with you. We'll help keep you safe."

Karma gave her a watery smile. "We'll keep each other safe."

Lily nodded and returned to her weaving, wiping at her eyes. "Is Ridge staying with us?" Lily didn't look up from her project, concentrating intensely on the task at hand.

"He says he is."

"Do you believe him?"

Karma took a moment to think back on their recent conversations and Ridge's actions since she had met him. He'd shown them time and again that he would be there. He'd said it, too. In her mind, though, actions spoke louder than words. "I think so."

Lily smiled at her answer. "I think so, too." She bumped Karma with her shoulder. "Is he your *boyfriend?*" she asked in a sing-song voice.

Karma laughed, nudging her back.

"Yes!" Ridge shouted, opening the bulkhead doors and entering the room. He dropped some herbs on the table and made a beeline for Karma, dropping a kiss on her lips and laughing when she placed her hands on her face to cover the heat on her cheeks.

Peter blushed in the doorway, but he had a grin on his face.

Ridge held out his hand to help her off the couch and led her into their bedroom. He closed the door behind them and pulled her into him, kissing her hard. He was out of breath when he pulled away and took a purposeful step back. "I left Peter at the garden and headed back toward town. They're hunting us. The goon squad must be clearing block by block. I backtracked to some of the areas between Phoenix Corps and my old place. They'd trashed them, too." He clenched his hands into fists, the knuckles turning white with the pressure. "I found a few people I helped relocate from the trailer park and told them to pack up and move farther out. They are going to catch up to us eventually, unless we leave Fairway entirely."

Karma sank onto the edge of the mattress, lowering her head. "I swore I wasn't going to leave until I shut that facility down." She looked down at her trembling hands. "I've failed."

Ridge was on his knees in front of her before she registered his movement, his hands on her face, forcing her to meet his determined gaze. "You didn't fail. Look at what you built at the trailer park. The family you built with Lily, Peter, Rosie, and Mrs. Thorn. And now, me."

"I can't keep everyone safe anymore."

"We'll keep them safe together now."

"We can't stay here." Defeat laced each word.

"Not forever, no. But they are a long way from here. We'll be careful, and I'll scout routes to get us out the safest way possible."

Karma hid her worry and stepped out of the bedroom. She'd keep their routine as normal as possible until it was time to move; there was no sense in worrying the kids before she had to.

After several more days, mostly fever-free, Karma felt stronger and ventured out into the hazy day to soak up a bit of sun. The fevers she experienced recently were low-grade and, while tiring, weren't as scary. The four of them walked around the new neighborhood, checking traps and familiarizing themselves with the lay of the land. They were surprised and delighted to find squirrels in two of their traps and a rabbit in one of the others. Nature was reclaiming the once prosperous city.

Ridge peeled off and headed back toward Phoenix Corps to see how much farther the raids had gotten, while Karma and the kids trained. Peter had thrived under Ridge's teaching. He was close to gaining the upper hand on Lily a few times. Karma wasn't strong enough yet to participate in the training, but she was able to coach, adjusting their forms as Peter and Lily sparred with each other.

They had a special feast that night, featuring the fresh meat from the traps, which had been seasoned perfectly with herbs from their thriving garden.

Karma smiled as Peter bounced in his chair, talking about how he helped with both growing the herbs and chopping them for the meal. He was so proud and blossoming under Ridge's attention.

After a dizzy spell while taking her dishes to the sink, she was banished to the couch to watch while the others cleaned up. The three of them joked around, splashing water at each other and horsing around. Lily and Peter had to grow up too fast, and their lighthearted moments were few and far between. But Ridge seemed to bring out happiness in all of them.

Still laughing and slightly damp, Ridge plopped on the couch next to her and tugged her against him, smiling at the kids' antics.

"Thank you for helping them be kids again for a bit," Karma whispered so only he could hear.

"It's good to see them smile more." He pressed his lips to her temple. "Still no fever today?"

She shook her head. "Fewer dizzy spells, too. I feel stronger, steadier on my feet, the last few days too."

"Good." He tucked her in closer and rested his cheek against the top of her head.

Contentment slid over her, a warm blanket of happiness cocooning her from the evil lurking outside their door.

Chapter 10

7619

Ridge

Karma's breathing evened out.

Ridge wasn't sure what he'd done in his life to deserve her, but he would savor each moment. The kids played a card game at the little table for a while, then retreated to their rooms. They all took advantage of the privacy they hadn't had in a long time. It was the safest and most comfortable place they would be for a while.

The raids from the goon squad were moving faster than he thought they would. They'd managed to rummage through three whole blocks from his place in the last few days. At that rate, they'd find this place in a few weeks.

Karma's hand slid to his thigh, and her sleepy eyes blinked up at him. "What's wrong?"

"I didn't mean to wake you."

"What's wrong?" she repeated. Karma shifted her weight and turned to face him. "How close are they?"

"We should be fine for a few weeks. I want you to regain as much strength as you can before we start moving. It could be a while before we find a good place to settle."

"They can't keep doing this to people." The vehemence in her voice held more strength than it had for weeks. "I'm tired of hiding. I'm tired of running."

"You're in no condition…"

"Yeah. I know," she snapped.

"Not just you. The kids, too."

"I know." The defeat in her tone pierced his heart. "I've spent years stealing from them to survive, gathering as much knowledge of their interworking as possible. And we managed to do more damage on the way out last time than I'd managed in the entire six years since I escaped."

"We damaged them on the way out, yes. But you managed to steal countless people from them. You saved those people from becoming what we are, from being glorified slaves to Phoenix Corps."

"A—I didn't save them all, and B—from becoming what *you* are. I'm no longer Altered." Karma shook her head. "I hated what they did to me, but now that it's gone, I'm struggling with being useless."

"You're not useless. Your help may be different now, but it's not useless."

Karma was quiet for a bit, her hand running up and down his thigh, distracting him. He could almost feel the gears in her mind turning and sat still, doing his best to ignore the maddening movements, allowing her that time. He clenched his teeth and closed his eyes. He wanted to reach for her, take her to their room.

At the abrupt halting of her hand, he opened his eyes, staring into her haunted grey ones.

"Pip said they were supplying the government with soldiers. With Altereds. He said Andrew Phoenix had so much influence that he might as well be the president. Phoenix Corps is bigger than we know, he said. We need more information. How big is it really? Did Pip exaggerate? There have to be records of it somehow. Phoenix Corps receives its supplies, which are intended for the people of Fairway, by barge. Those supplies have to be coming from somewhere. Do the people sending the supplies know what Phoenix Corps is doing here? Would they even care if they did know? Is some of that information in the records Malcolm wanted me to get? How do we take out something so big? We don't have an army. We have two kids, an Altered, and whatever the hell I am now."

"We take one piece at a time. It's like the wooden tower game. If you take enough pieces from the base, it will topple. Maybe we consider meeting with Malcolm again? That's a decision we will make together." Ridge placed his hand on the back of her neck, caressing the soft skin there with his fingers. "You displaced a lot of their pieces over the years. We rocked the foundation on our way out when we blew up the loading docks. I don't see why we can't make a few more waves before we get the hell out of this place." Ridge dropped his head to hers. "Whatever the hell you are now, huh? Whatever you are is *mine.*"

Chapter 11

5713

Karma

Karma snuck out of bed before the sun rose, careful not to wake Ridge. She took a quick moment to stare at his sleeping figure. He was as much hers as she was his. Whatever it took, she'd do everything in her power to make sure they were all safe.

Karma made her way to the bulkhead doors. The doors, and her body, groaned at the effort it took to raise the door and lock it into place. Frost blanketed the grass and crunched under her feet. Her breath puffed out in a white cloud in the cold air, and she hugged her arms to her body. She didn't like the cold before she became Altered and liked it even less after. The latest serum hadn't made it any better.

The grass snapped audibly with the hard frost as she trekked through the backyard and worked her way into the lightly wooded area beyond. The dull light starting to peek through the trees showed the leaves beginning their change.

Karma dragged her hand over the rough bark of one of the trees, letting the grit scrape at her skin as she walked on. Vines and vegetation hung from the canopy and grasped at her while she weaved her way through. Under the cover of the trees, the frost had not yet reached the ground, but the dead leaves from previous seasons continued to crunch beneath her feet.

The trees thickened, and she was no longer able to see the house behind her. Still, she walked on. Despite the shade of the trees, it felt warmer here than it had when she was in the yard. A break in the trees wasn't far off. Curious as to what lay on the other side, she headed to the slightly brighter light ahead.

Stopping next to one of the last trees, a massive fissure opened just beyond her feet. She couldn't see the bottom, and it was at least twenty feet wide. There must have been more of the neighborhood on the other side of that fissure at one time. A couple of charred chimneys stood in the distance, but nature had reclaimed the rest of the area.

"Don't approach the edge. It's not stable."

Karma jumped at Ridge's voice. She hadn't heard him move through the leaves blanketing the forest floor. His warmth cocooned around her as he pulled her to him, his arms circling her, coming to rest low on her stomach.

"Is there a way to get across here?"

"You'd probably have to go miles in either direction." The rumble of his voice vibrated against her back. "How are you this morning?"

"I did the walk without much trouble. And, I haven't noticed a fever."

"I worried when you were gone without a word."

"Sorry." She turned in his warmth, facing him. "It's going to get cold. That basement is going to get cold. Too cold for the kids."

"We won't be able to stay much longer anyway."

"You said there were more clothes in the truck that we stole on the way out of Phoenix Corps last time, right?"

"Yeah. I have those stashed away. I was planning to grab the food later today."

"I can carry clothes. I'll go with you."

"You walked a long way this morning."

She pressed a kiss to his lips. "I'm feeling better right now. I'll rest a bit when we get back, before we head out."

Late afternoon approached. Karma and Ridge wove their way over and around the debris-filled streets and alleyways. Ridge constantly checked with her to make sure she wasn't too tired. After the hundredth time, Karma stopped and grabbed his hand. "I'll let you know if I am tiring out. Right now, I'm fine. Relax, please. There are other things you should be paying attention to right now."

He looked her over closely one more time, then turned and kept moving.

Ridge scented the air, giving her updates on what he had picked up in each new location.

They were five blocks from Ridge's place when he veered to the left and led her into a mostly collapsed building and down a set of stairs. She wasn't sure how those steps held her weight, let alone Ridge's. They looked like they were held together with spit and a wish. In the basement, earth poured in from the crumbling walls, and most of the debris from the building above now resided here. She doubted there was more than twenty square feet of open space in the room.

Ridge pointed to several boxes under the stairs. "Stuff what you can into bags. I'm going to collect food from another place a few doors down. I'll be back in a few minutes."

Karma worked quickly, pulling clothes for each of them. Nothing was super thick, but they could wear a few layers to ward off the cold, at least a bit.

By the time she finished, the four bags she brought were packed tight. She heaved the bags over her shoulders and crossed her fingers that the stairs would hold her.

Ridge still wasn't back.

The light was waning, and they'd need to head back soon; it was a long walk back.

A scraping sound caught her attention first; boots dragging over a wooden floor. Voices reached her next.

Karma tucked her bags under a precariously leaning brick wall and crept into the alleyway. She peered around the corner.

Three of the goon squad members stood watching, while two others dragged Ridge by his arms, which were zip-tied behind his back.

Karma's head swiveled, looking around for anything she could use for a weapon. She hadn't brought her walking stick because she knew her hands would be full on the way back. Spotting a hunk of rebar sticking out of a broken-down section of wall, Karma grabbed it with both hands and pulled.

It didn't budge.

She frantically scanned for something else, but everything else worth using was too big for her to lift. If she could just get this piece of rebar to break free…

Karma closed her eyes, clamped down on her jaw, adjusted her grip, and pulled with everything she had. One minute she was pulling, and the next, her arms windmilled as she tried to regain her balance, rebar in hand. She caught her balance and rushed back to the corner.

The two men were now dragging Ridge down the street. The three spectators, two men and a woman, stood with their chests puffed out and their arms crossed. A wicked-looking gash along one of the guy's necks wept blood. The third guy adjusted his stance, and he favored his left leg. The movement opened up a tear in his pants, revealing a gash on his thigh. She didn't think the woman's eyes were shaded by her protruding forehead; she sported a black eye in the making.

She gripped the rebar tighter and sprinted into the street. The element of surprise was on her side, and she swung the rebar like a bat, catching the guy with the neck gash under his chin, snapping his head back and knocking him to the ground.

The guy with the torn pants whipped out a knife and charged.

Karma swung the rebar back down to block the knife. While she was a second too late, the rebar connected with the top of his hand. The sound of his wail almost drowned out the sound of the bones in his hand shattering. She readjusted her weight, driving her elbow back into the ribs of the woman who'd gotten behind her, then stabbed forward with the rebar, driving it like a spear into the goon whose hand she broke.

She let go of the rebar, twisting around, driving her elbow into the face of the woman behind her, yanking the rebar, with the opposite hand, out of the goon's guts, and spinning it around, cracking it into the woman's ribs. The rod slipped from her hands, clattering against the cracked asphalt at her feet.

The woman staggered back, wheezing, coughing up blood.

Karma snap kicked the woman in the stomach.

Arms thrown out to the sides, the woman tried to catch herself, but flew ass over teakettle over a partial wall, and into the building they'd dragged Ridge from.

One of the men charged her, catching her in the gut with his shoulder like a linebacker and driving her backward into the shell of a rusted-out car. It forced the air from her lungs, and stars danced in her vision. Karma brought her elbows down on his spine, kneeing him in the chest at the same time.

He gasped for air.

The first guy she knocked down staggered to his feet, his jaw offset at a strange angle and missing several teeth. A knife slipped into his hand.

Karma grabbed the man whose shoulder was still embedded in her stomach by the waistband of his pants, jerking up and toward her. The first guy's knife sank into the back of the other man's thigh as he brought it down at her. She shoved outward, using him as a shield and a battering ram.

More scuffling reached her ears, but she couldn't pay attention to it.

The woman was back on her feet, entering the fray with the other two men. The only one who wasn't moving was the guy she'd stabbed with the rebar.

Her energy waned as the first guy got back to his feet.

He roared and pounded his chest like a gorilla. The roar was muffled since his mouth wouldn't move right.

Karma didn't see the woman charge her with the knife until it was almost too late. She shoved her right arm into the path of the knife and felt the skin separate as the blade scored her forearm, and she grabbed the wrist holding the knife, slamming it against the window frame of the car until the knife dropped inside. Karma stomped on the bent end of the rebar, flipping it off the pavement and into her hand, striking out at the woman.

It cracked into the woman's upper arm, the shock reverberating down the metal shaft. Karma's fingers, aching with fatigue, barely held onto it.

Exhaustion dragged at her. She needed to end this fight, and soon. Her vision tunneled. Karma grabbed a fistful of the woman's hair and slammed her face into the car frame three times, kicking her away again. Turning to refocus on the other men, she saw Ridge standing over them, his wrists still tied behind his back, blood and dirt streaked down his face. His breathing was labored, and a slice near his ear had tufts of his panther hair sticking through, giving him an odd-looking sideburn.

No one else moved.

Karma staggered to Ridge, searching for severe injuries.

"Cut the ties." He shifted his arms, indicating the zip ties still locked tightly around his wrists. The ties had bitten into his skin with his movements, slicing through, exposing more tufts of hair poking through.

Karma snapped up one of the knives dropped on the ground, placing it between the zip tie and Ridge's wrists. She pulled until the plastic snapped.

He spun, running his hands over her, assessing her.

"I'm just tired. No permanent damage," she assured him.

He gathered her carefully to him. "Thanks for saving my ass again."

Ridge was trying for humor, but tears filled Karma's eyes. She refused to let them fall but held onto him tighter.

He tapped her on the shoulder, and she raised her watery gaze to him. Ridge struggled to pull in a full breath, and Karma released her hold.

Ridge raised her forearm and turned it. Osteoderms were visible in the gaping cut on her forearm. He took her by the hand. "Squeeze my hand."

When she did as he asked, Ridge's eyes widened, and he raised up on his toes, tapping her shoulder as he clenched his jaw.

"Your strength is back." The awe in his voice was evident.

Chapter 12

7619

Ridge

He'd been woozy and disoriented as those two goon squad members started dragging him away. It had taken all five of them to overpower him. Originally, the sounds of fighting hadn't registered until one of the assholes holding him lifted him back onto his feet and shoved Ridge into the other guy, taking off toward the sounds of the scrum. Ridge looked up.

Karma was outnumbered four-to-one.

Ridge slammed his head back, feeling the satisfying crack of the goon's nose and feeling the warm blood from it oozing down his neck and back. He mule kicked the goon in the knee, satisfied when it bent the wrong way, the howl of pain behind him making Ridge's ears ring.

The goon's arms banded tightly around his chest, probably to hold himself upright as much as to restrain Ridge. The pressure made it hard to pull in air, and his vision sparkled.

Throwing his weight forward, the goon grappled for purchase but ultimately lost his grip and flew over Ridge's head, landing hard on his neck. The sound of breaking bone reached his ears as Ridge hit the ground face-first, unable to stop his own momentum.

He rolled to his side and awkwardly got to his feet. Ridge pulled at the offending ties clamping his arms together behind his back, but couldn't get the leverage needed to break them.

Ridge barreled toward the goon squad members fighting Karma.

The largest guy was on his feet. He held his jaw at a strange angle, and blood dripped from it.

Ridge charged him, driving his shoulder into the big guy's side, hearing bone breaking under the pressure and speed of the hit. Ridge shifted his weight as the guy hit the ground and rolled to his feet. He spun, kicking out with his heavy boot at the guy's temple.

A glance to the side told him Karma still stood on her feet against the lone female goon.

The other goon who'd tried to drag him away struggled to get to his feet. The handle of a knife stuck out from the back of his thigh. Ridge kicked out, dislodging the knife from the goon's leg. It clattered to the ground, and blood spurted from the wound. The blade must have nicked a major artery. The goon's face paled, and he dropped to his knee. Ridge kicked out again, connecting with his chest and knocking him backwards. He didn't get back up.

Threat gone, he turned to help Karma, but the woman she'd fought lay at her feet.

Karma turned, ready to take on another fight, the relief on her face obvious when she saw him standing over the others. She stumbled forward, exhaustion mingling with the relief he read in her expression. Her hands ran over his body, searching for injury.

Ridge turned, holding his arms awkwardly to the side, asking her to cut away the bindings.

Karma grabbed a knife from the ground and sliced through the ties.

Free to move, he spun, taking his time to search her for injury. A long gash cut through the tattoo on her forearm, and when he gathered her into his arms, she held on with a strength that could crack his ribs. Ridge tapped on her shoulder to get her to loosen her hold. He couldn't get in enough air to speak. Adrenaline, maybe?

Karma stepped back, then squeezed his fingers like he asked. He instinctively moved up and away, trying to get away from the pressure and pain. "Your strength is back," he said in awe.

She turned then and surveyed the carnage they'd left in the street. Her eyes were wide when they turned back to him. She stared down at her, now shaking, hands and her breathing picked back up.

Ridge gathered her in his arms and lifted, bringing her out of the street and into the hidden cove of the building where he'd kept their supplies. He sat on the crate he intended to use for carrying supplies and sat her on his lap, holding her while she processed the events.

Keeping his ears peeled for anything unusual, Ridge caressed her back. His ears alerted him to the goon squad they'd just taken out, before they'd gotten the jump on him. It's the reason this cove and their supplies remained hidden. They'd need to get out of here soon, but she needed to be okay first.

"Was it just adrenaline?" she asked quietly, mirroring his thoughts from earlier.

He paused in thought before speaking. "I didn't think about it earlier, but you opened the bulkhead door this morning."

"Yeah. I know it's heavy, but…"

"Karma, the kids can't open or close it *together*. There's half a freaking tree attached to it."

"But whatever they gave me…"

"Maybe it's finally working its way out of your system."

He gave her a minute to think about that before standing, guiding her down his body to stand on her own. He took her in a deep kiss, then forced himself to step back and away. They needed to get moving. "It's getting dark, and we shouldn't stick around here. Are you up for the walk back?"

She nodded and grabbed a few cans from the makeshift shelf in the cove, handing them to him to place in the crate they'd been sitting on.

The crate was full, and the shelves were empty a few minutes later.

"Are you okay to carry that?" she asked, her hand caressing the broken skin in front of his ear.

"I've got it. Let's get out of here before someone comes looking for these assholes."

Karma nodded and led the way out of the cove.

Peter was already in his room asleep by the time they made it back to the neighborhood. Lily, however, waited up until they were safely back in the basement.

Karma handed Lily a bag of clothes and quietly placed another just inside Peter's room. She took the other two bags into their room and didn't emerge.

Karma had been quiet for most of the walk, and Ridge wanted to touch her, connect with her, but too much danger lurked in the darkness, and he needed to keep his senses peeled. He set down the box of supplies in the kitchen area, bid Lily goodnight, and headed into the bedroom, a first aid kit in his hands.

She sat on the edge of the bed, staring at her hands.

Without speaking, Ridge took her right hand and turned it over, exposing the gash running from nearly her elbow to her wrist. The osteoderms of her Komodo dragon skin clicked against his nails. The brown-green-grey color of them reminded him of rough stone. The slice divided the P and C of her tattoo. Ridge carefully cleaned it out and used butterfly bandages to hold the human skin together over the osteoderms until it could heal on its own.

That done, Ridge examined the bruises forming on her other arm and along her jaw where she must have taken a punch.

"I'm fine."

"I'll be the judge of that," he replied, continuing his exam.

Karma grabbed his hand, trapping it in hers, and waited until their eyes met. "I'm fine. You got the worst of it." Her feather-soft touch glided over the slice near his ear and picked up butterfly bandages to tend to his wounds. She took the time to examine him, just as he had, and trailed soft kisses over each wound and bruise as she finished tending it.

His eyes closed at the tentative touch of her mouth on his when she finished. He gripped her hips and pulled her against him—the need for her rising ever higher.

Her breathing increased, her fingers tightening in his hair as his lips trailed down her jaw onto her neck.

Ridge turned, rolling her onto her back beneath him, keeping his weight off her with one arm, the other hand sliding beneath the hem of her shirt. The smooth skin was cool to his touch, the muscles beneath trembling with each pass of his fingers.

Karma tugged at his hair, pulling his lips back to hers.

Her hands roamed his body, and she rolled, forcing him onto his back.

He gripped her hips, holding her in place where she straddled him. His fingers, unable to remain still, massaged the skin above the waistband of her jeans. The vision of her, four-on-one, came flooding back, and his grip tightened on her.

Karma paused in her inspection of each of his bruises and cuts, a question in her eyes.

"You should have run. You should have left me and come back to the kids, gotten them out of here."

She echoed his words back to him. "I'm not going anywhere." She touched her forehead to his and closed her eyes. "You're stuck with me now."

Her eyes opened, emotion swirling within as tears threatened to spill over.

Lifting his head to the junction of her neck and shoulder, he filled his lungs with her scent, warmth, and comfort cocooning around him. His voice cracked as he spoke. "You didn't know you had your strength back. You didn't know you could fight them off. There were too many of them…"

Karma smiled down at him. "Someone once told me that I taught Lily to fight, even knowing she wasn't Altered, to keep her safe." She pulled him up for a kiss. "She once faced off against an Altered. He got the upper hand, and I helped her out of the situation. If I did nothing else, I could've distracted them enough for you to get the upper hand. I didn't take all of them down without help."

Ridge growled. His arms tightened around her, wanting to protect her even still. The fact that they were safe now didn't matter. He'd keep her safe. Always.

He took his time with her this time, more time than ever before. Coaxing each sigh and gasp from her, he prolonged her pleasure. Ridge showed her with his actions how much she meant to him, until she lay trembling in his arms.

Chapter 13

Karma

She curled into Ridge's warmth, not wanting to get up yet. Feeling his muscles contract as her hand skimmed over his abdomen, his intense gaze on her when she lifted her face to his, Karma marveled at the feelings threatening to overwhelm her. Panic rose in her chest, and her mind spun. She struggled to pull in a full breath.

Ridge reacted instantly, rolling her onto her back, cooing soft sounds and words that weren't register-ing.

She closed her eyes against the onslaught of feelings and concentrated on his voice and gentle touch as he soothed her. Karma counted to ten slowly as she breathed in, and ten more as she exhaled.

Ridge's breathing synced up with hers, his breath fanning over her cheek and neck, distracting her with other delicious sensations. His eyes were softened with concern when she finally felt calm enough to open them.

"What happened?" he whispered.

Karma needed to ask the question that crept into her thoughts just before she panicked. Instead of looking into his eyes, exposing more of her vulnerability, she stared at a spot on the ceiling behind his ear. "With me stronger, able to protect the kids, when will you go?"

She pretended she didn't see the hurt flash over his face at the question.

"You want me to go?" he spoke his question slowly.

"You don't have to stay to protect the kids any longer."

"I never *had* to stay, Karma. I stayed because I want to, because I love you."

A sob ripped through her at his words.

Ridge backed away from her, his brow furrowed in confusion.

Karma threw her forearm over her eyes and curled her body into his, grasping his shirt to keep him from withdrawing. "I panicked," she said, answering his first question. She drew her arm back down, tentatively looking up at him. "In one moment, I realized how much I love you, and the next, I thought you wouldn't want to stay, since I can protect the kids again."

Ridge drew her into an unhurried, extended kiss, igniting every nerve ending in her body.

When he pulled away, he said, "I wasn't going anywhere before Phoenix Corps took you, and I'm certainly not going anywhere now that I know you feel the same. I told you before, you are stuck with me."

She dipped her head shyly.

"Hey," he said, lifting her chin, "The panic attack..."

"I had a few after Phoenix Corps had me the first time. I haven't had one in a while. I learned to cope. I think after the last experience with them, the worry about what was happening to me after they gave me that serum, and the intensity of what I'm feeling... it just overwhelmed me."

Karma sat on the plush couch, wrapped in several layers of clothes to ward off the chill, letting the warmth from the can of soup in her hands seep into her. Her mind wandered, lost in thought as Ridge sat beside her.

Lily and Peter, dressed in layers as well, sat in the two chairs at the small table, eating their soup and chatting quietly.

"What are you thinking about so hard over there?" Ridge asked.

Karma kept her voice quiet. "Malcolm and what could be in the files he stashed. Could it be the answer we've been waiting for? Or is it some elaborate ploy?"

Ridge's hand tightened on the can in his hand, denting it. His voice dropped to a menacing, gravelly timbre. "You think it's a trap?"

She reached over and squeezed his wrist, an offer of comfort, coaxing him to loosen up his grip. "I always think it could be a trap. Phoenix Corps destroyed more than my world. They ripped away any trust I had in people. I've learned to trust you, but you know how long that took. Jacob wouldn't work with Phoenix Corps ever again. His involvement makes me believe it is legit.

"Pip said Phoenix Corps is bigger than we know. On one hand, if the government is condoning it, is *anywhere* safe? On the other hand, if the files have evidence to take Phoenix Corps down, can we pass up the opportunity?"

His eyes narrowed, and he cocked his head as if listening. "When I was there, they brought in a lot of people. There weren't *that* many Altereds added to the goon squad at the time, though. How many didn't make it through the treatments? I never cared to find out those numbers, but it's safe to say that more people made it through than were then 'employed' by Phoenix Corps. And we know they don't alter someone and then let them walk out the door freely."

Karma nodded. "If we leave Fairway altogether, will we be any safer if they are really that important to the government?"

"It'll be a lot harder for them to find us in the expansive country than it would be in this town."

"But if they are that strong, how can just the two of us take them down?"

Ridge set their empty cans on the small table next to the couch and pulled her close. "Taking them down may be too big for us. But we can hurt them on the way out."

Karma rested her head on his strong shoulder and closed her eyes. The uncertainties of their future weighed on her. What would they find beyond the borders of Fairway? She'd sent lots of people there but had never ventured so far herself. Fairway was all she'd ever known before the quake. The only thing she'd known since. Life wasn't easy, but she knew how to survive here.

Ridge's hand stayed on her thigh, lazily moving back and forth. Since their first time together, he kept a physical connection between them whenever he had the opportunity to. She took comfort in that connection. She shouldered all the burdens for so long. When he touched her, she didn't feel alone anymore.

Chapter 14

Karma

It was no longer safe for either of them to get supplies on their own.

Ridge worked with Peter on his training, while Karma led Lily out and away from Phoenix Corps. They trekked out into the woods she'd gone through on her first exploration of their new neighborhood and headed along the deep fissure.

"What are we looking for?" Lily asked about an hour into their hike.

"We can't stay here. Phoenix Corps is looking for Ridge and me. They are canvassing each neighborhood, searching for us and probably taking anyone they find. Eventually, they will make it out this far. Fairway needs to be behind us sooner rather than later," Karma replied.

"You're really going to leave Fairway? Even being afraid?"

Karma stopped and turned, looking directly at Lily, keeping her full attention. "Being afraid is not enough to stop me from doing everything in my power to keep the two of you safe." She turned back in the direction they were heading and restarted her steps.

"Where will we go?"

"That's one of the things we are looking for," Karma said, bumping her shoulder against Lily's.

"Really?"

Karma nodded. "Tell me what you see when you look over there." She pointed across the fissure.

"Grasses and vines covering every surface it can. Charred remains peeking through in spots."

"Beyond that."

"Beyond that?" she asked, squinting her eyes, peering into the distance. "I don't know. It could be anything."

"Correct. It could be anything. We don't know what we will find once we cross this fissure. We are about to head into the unknown. It could be a paradise with no more scavenging, back to the old days of shopping in an actual store for food and clothes. Reliable power and water at our fingertips. Or it could be a wasteland. None of us will know until we venture that far."

Lily's eyes widened.

"How far will we have to go?"

Karma shrugged.

Lily kicked a rock with the toe of her shoe, sending it tumbling into the deep ravine.

"We'll learn about the new place just the same as we learned this one. It may take time. But Ridge and I will make sure that you and Peter are taken care of, I promise."

"Ridge is coming too?"

Karma couldn't stop the heat she felt rising in her cheeks. "Yes. Ridge is coming, too."

Lily threw her arms around Karma and squealed. "He's really staying!"

They acted like schoolgirls, celebrating for a moment, then Karma bumped Lily with her hip. "Okay, time to go. We've dallied enough. Let's keep following the fissure for a bit and see where it leads us.

Karma wondered if it would ever end. They crossed over roads shorn through, with one side shifted a hundred yards or more to the west. The charred shell of a gas station stood on their side of the gaping fissure, and what must have been the area with the pumps was a massive crater on the other side, a good way down. Karma shuddered, remembering the smell when those tanks exploded.

About a mile past the gas station, the fissure narrowed. As she looked farther south, she could see it open back up again, but here, it was narrow.

Karma motioned to Lily to stay back, and she crept toward the edge, testing its stability, scrambling back and away when a five-foot section of the earth dropped away, plummeting into the depths. "Well, that's not going to be our escape route."

"How did you get the others out?" Lily asked. The color had drained from her face.

"The river on the north end of town."

"Can we go that way?"

"The best place to cross the river is where the barges come in. That's where I started 'shopping' after escaping. They *really* didn't like me stealing from there. Massive amounts of security measures were put into place. And, as far as I've been able to tell, over the years, they haven't lessened the measures at all. The next closest place is a couple of miles away, around a bend in the river. Far enough that their security doesn't reach, but it's closer to the main facility. I'd rather not take you and Peter that close to Phoenix Corps, if we can help it." Karma shook her head. "But we may not have a choice. We'll scout the other direction tomorrow. For now, let's head back."

Darkness neared, and Ridge paced as they set foot back in the neighborhood. Karma was impressed with Lily's ability to keep so quiet in their hike back that Ridge didn't hear them until they reached the very edge of the trees.

"I was worried."

"Sorry. We walked down to the gas station near Pine Street. There's no good place to cross. We'll work our way up the other side tomorrow."

"Is the river going to be the best bet?" he asked.

"Maybe. But let's check out the other end of the fissure first."

Lily trotted across the yard and into the basement, leaving Karma and Ridge in the growing darkness.

"How are you feeling?" Ridge asked, bending down to look her in the eye.

"Tired. Frustrated. Worried."

He pulled her into his arms, and she felt some of it slip away. "It feels like it will be a warmer night than the last few."

"Hopefully it sticks around for a bit." She held on to Ridge like he was the lifeline she'd been missing. "We need to get out of here before the weather changes too much."

"Are you thinking about meeting up with Malcolm before we go?"

"I don't think we have a choice. I can't just walk away now."

She felt his nod against her hair and tightened her fists in his shirt. "If we want to get information to take to the government or media, assuming they still exist outside of Fairway, I don't think we have a choice but to help Malcolm get his files. But, can we trust him?"

"That's the million-dollar question, isn't it?"

Chapter 15

Ridge

The sun was barely peeking over the horizon when Ridge made his way into the backyard.

He heard Karma before her scent washed over him and her arms wrapped around him from behind, snuggling in. Ridge placed his warm hands over her cooler ones and squeezed lightly.

"The kids are up and moving around. What is your plan for the day?" she asked.

"Why don't you and Lily head along the other side of the fissure today, and Peter and I will work here around the property. Maybe tonight you and I can sneak away to spy on what's going on with the goon squad. See how far they've made it. We should get as close to Phoenix Corps as possible, see how far they are with the repairs, and scout the best ways in and out."

Karma nodded her head against his back. "The walks are helping me regain my stamina. Lily is learning to move quietly and taking in everything she can about her surroundings. She's picking up the skills quickly."

"Peter is doing well in his training, too. He's come close to getting the upper hand on Lily several times now."

Karma's arms tightened around him. "If something happens to us, they'll be strong enough to make it. Right?"

Ridge stepped forward enough to turn and wrap her in his arms, pulling her tight against him and resting his cheek against the top of her head. "You've taught them to stand on their own two feet. If anyone is strong enough, it's those two kids."

They stood there for several long moments. Ridge was lost in thought about all the dangers that they faced over the last few months, and the ones they were soon going to walk into. He didn't know what would come from the next steps they took, but he was glad to have her stand with him, walking with him into the unknown. He'd protect her and the kids no matter what it took.

His grip involuntarily tightened on her for a moment, then he stepped back. "We should go have breakfast before we venture out today."

Karma linked their hands as she turned to head back to the house.

The peacefulness would be short-lived, but Ridge would savor each moment as it came.

Karma and Lily returned from their trek along the fissure. Karma carried some freshly caught squirrels, handing them off to Peter to clean, then grabbed Ridge by the hand and pulled him into their room.

"There's a spot, maybe eight miles away, that seems to be narrow and stable enough for us to get across. The gap is about five feet. There are several buildings partially intact on our side of the fissure. We could scavenge some boards to build a makeshift bridge."

Encouraged, he sat on the edge of the bed, pulling her down next to him. "Let's have dinner with the kids and then check out the progress of the goon squad tonight. Then we will have a better grasp of the timeline." His thumb rubbed over the back of her hand.

"The kids will want to come along. Lily already talked about it while we were out. I think they should stay behind."

"I agree."

"After what we encountered last time..."

Ridge turned her chin, making her look at him. "I agree. They are even better trained now than they were, but going against Altereds is still above their skill. Will probably always be above their skill."

"She'll want to follow us."

"We'll close the bulkhead doors, so they can't."

"If something happens and we don't come back?"

His brow furrowed, and he grimaced. He hadn't thought about that. "Will Lily stay put if we tell her to?"

"I hope the experience of not following directions and getting scooped up by the goon squad last time will be enough to scare her into obeying this time."

Ridge and Karma, dressed head to toe in layers of black, stole out into the night.

The crisp air bit at the exposed flesh on his face. They were in for another night of frost. Patches of the ground were already slick. It didn't take as long as before for them to reach the outskirts of the city with Karma's improved stamina. It felt warmer here with more concrete and asphalt to absorb the mild warmth of the day. They slowed their pace, checking each area thoroughly before moving to the next, as more places to hide heightened the danger. In too few blocks, the telltale scents of the goon squad appeared.

Karma turned away from the area and headed parallel to their location, further east of the city. Ridge followed her, his ears peeled for sounds she may not hear.

They worked their way into the trailer park, but no evidence of Jacob, Malcolm, or anyone else registered. The goon squad hadn't returned either, as far as he could tell.

He followed her through alleyways and down streets. They entered a small park, weaving their way through the overgrown foliage to the still broken fence line and onto Phoenix Corps property. They kept to the fence, staying hidden by the darkness and trees.

"The guard shack is still in pieces," Karma whispered, pointing to the area of the main gate.

Ridge pointed to the area just beyond. "The guards are posted there. They've just been standing in the open. And, they have doubled the number of them on duty at any given time." He shifted his hand, pointing up to the loading docks. "The scaffolding is still up on the door we drove through. They've taken down the rest in the last few weeks or so. They are almost back to full functioning."

Karma gave a frustrated huff, then turned and headed back the way they'd come.

Chapter 16

Karma

A chill ran down Karma's back as she looked across Finley Avenue into the darkness beyond. It seemed no light could penetrate the darkness. But this would be the best way to find Jacob or Malcolm. Ridge stood at her back, a strong, steady, and supportive presence. He didn't question her sanity as she stepped away from the fence and followed her nose.

A mild sweetness in the air pulled her further into the darkness. It seemed an odd smell, considering their location. Rot and refuse permeated most of the air, but she followed the scent trail easily.

Ridge's hand grabbed onto the back of her shirt, pulling her against him and indicating an area to their right where he'd heard something she'd missed. She paused and waited for him to relax his grip before continuing down the street, over and around a few dilapidated cars and into a blind alley. The rancid smell threatened to overwhelm her, but she picked up the thread of sweetness remaining and focused on it.

Karma turned sideways, inching her way between two large dumpsters.

The alleyway was narrow. The dumpsters wouldn't have been placed directly across from one another this way unless someone was trying to keep people out.

Ridge had to stop, unable to squeeze through, and she held up a hand to keep him from moving one of the dumpsters so he could fit.

She stepped between the dumpsters, and the next few moments were a blur of movement and noise.

An arm shot out of the darkness, pinning her against the crumbling, rough brick wall to one side of the alley. That sweet smell engulfed her.

A strange, cat-like scream emitted from Ridge's throat as he vaulted the dumpsters, knocking the offending arm away and the body along with it. He turned his back to her, placing himself as a shield. His claws glinted, catching light from somewhere, and blood dripped from one of them. "Mine."

The spindly man, the source of the sweet scent, scurried back and away, whimpering and cradling his now bleeding limb. Jacob.

Karma wrapped the bottom of Ridge's shirt in her fist, holding him in place, stopping any further attack. Then, she placed her other palm on the center of his back. "He's no threat," she whispered.

Ridge spared her an incredulous glance, then returned his stare to the man curled against the opposite wall of the alleyway. A snarl marred his usually handsome face.

She stepped to the side but was immediately pushed back against the wall by Ridge's weight. His body blocked her view of the man on the ground. "He's no threat," she repeated, louder this time.

He shifted his weight, pushing her harder into the wall. When she tried to maneuver her way around him, he snarled *at her*.

Karma relaxed her body, and after his body relaxed in answer, she plowed the front of her knee into the back of his. The contact caught him off guard, and he stumbled forward, leaving space for her to step around him.

He regained his footing, but not before she reversed the tables, using her body to hold his in place.

She knew he was strong enough; he could lift her out of the way, but Ridge simply placed his hands at her hips and held her there, keeping her from stepping toward the cowering man. Karma lowered her body until she was crouched in front of Ridge, at eye level with Jacob.

"We're not going to hurt you, Jacob," Karma said softly.

His eyes flicked up to Ridge and back.

"He thought you were going to hurt me. But you and I know you won't, right?"

Jacob grunted.

Ridge tightened his hands on her shoulders and tugged up, trying to get her to stand, but she stayed where she was.

"Can I see your arm? Help you?"

He looked about to refuse.

Karma reached her hand out, palm down, hand relaxed, like she was approaching an injured animal.

"I'll help you wrap it, and we'll go. We won't come back here."

Jacob's eyes skirted up to Ridge, who remained quiet. His lip curled in a sneer, but he nodded. "He stays here."

"Fat chance…"

Karma held up a hand, stopping Ridge in mid-protest. "He can follow us to your first aid supplies but stay outside." She squeezed his hand when he was about to protest again.

Jacob looked from her to Ridge and back again, then nodded.

When she stepped forward to help Jacob to his feet, he jerked back and then shoved her with his uninjured arm. Ridge's hand shot out, but Karma caught it before it connected with Jacob. "Back up and give him room to stand." She backed herself into Ridge, making him take several steps back. She felt the rumble of the growl in Ridge's chest as it vibrated against her back.

Jacob scanned the area warily, as if looking for others.

"It's just Ridge and me."

When Jacob finally continued down the alleyway, Ridge kept close to Karma, brushing against her with every step. At the same time, his head stayed on a swivel, studying the dilapidated buildings for any sign of danger.

Every third step, Jacob kicked a stone. It would ping off an object, and then he would repeat. Step, step, scrape, ping. Down each road and alley.

Ridge's low growl rumbled, and he reached out, pulling Karma to a stop.

"Keep moving," Jacob ordered.

Ridge bristled.

Karma slid her hand into his, pulling him forward a step.

In a flash, Ridge switched their positions, placing himself between her and whatever danger he had noticed.

"I said, keep *moving!*" Jacob whisper-shouted, turning around, stomping his foot for emphasis.

Karma heard the panic in Jacob's voice. She felt eyes on her now, raising the small hairs on the back of her neck. "Follow him, please."

Ridge moved to follow Jacob, his head and eyes never stopping as he surveyed the broken-down buildings and darkness all around them.

Metal clattered against asphalt down an alley to her right, and Jacob sped up, scurrying over the shell of an old, burnt-out car and into another alleyway. Again, the dumpsters were angled, making it impossible for most people to get through without moving them and creating a lot of racket in the process—a great early warning system.

Jacob bent his body at odd angles as he maneuvered his way past the dumpsters. Karma, not nearly as rail-thin as Jacob, struggled but managed to get through without making too much noise. Ridge bypassed the dumpsters by vaulting over, landing on his feet between Karma and Jacob before she had cleared the last of the maze.

"Stay," Jacob ordered Ridge like he was a dog.

Karma quickly put herself between the men, pulling Ridge's eyes to her with her hand on his cheek. "I won't be long."

She turned sharply. "That was disrespectful and uncalled for. Do anything like that again, and you can figure out a way to dress your own damn wound."

Jacob glared at her, but turned and wormed his way through a door, disguised behind half of a fallen wall. He didn't speak as he grabbed a box of first aid supplies from beneath a broken sink. He sat stoically, staring at the doorway, while she cleaned and bandaged the deep wound.

"He'll stay outside, like you asked. You don't need to stare a hole through your door."

"Hrumpf."

Karma shrugged and continued her ministrations until the wound was clean and bandaged. She stood and picked up the discarded supplies. "We can help you across the river, if you want. The goon squad is canvassing all the areas in the city, looking for Ridge and me. They'll eventually come here."

"No, they won't."

"It's naive of you to think that. But it's your choice, Jacob." Karma headed for the door, stopping with her hand on the knob. "Pip is dead. We killed him on the way out of Phoenix Corps, right before Ridge *helped you* evacuate the trailer park. While he is no longer a threat, I'm sure it didn't take long for Phoenix Corps to replace him."

Jacob sat in silence, staring at a smear of dirt on the wall in front of him, as if it were a fine piece of art he was studying.

"Why don't you want to leave?"

"They want me to stay." His tone brought chills to her skin, and the way he swung his eyes to hers had her backing away from the door.

Chapter 17

7619

Ridge

Ridge stood with his back to the wall Karma and Jacob slipped under. Aware of eyes watching him from many directions, he kept still and pretended to be bored and unconcerned. He feigned ignorance as three people eased into the alley, one from each end, and one from above, creeping down the rickety fire escape, barely holding on to the side of the building in front of him.

The woman approaching from above was smaller in weight and stature. She was too far away, and the slight breeze didn't carry her scent in his direction, but he guessed from the silhouette that the woman was Allie. The two failing to sneak into the alley had the look of goon squad members. Duke entered from the right side of the alley, Meg from the left, converging in the center, on either side of the fire escape.

A fourth person peeked around the corner of the alley where Duke was—the scrawny pencil-pusher, Malcolm.

With the barest movements, Ridge adjusted his weight. He kept his hands relaxed and tracked their movements with his eyes. He hoped Karma would stay inside. There was no telling what these people wanted, and he wasn't about to let her be in danger. It already rankled that she was inside without him. He didn't trust Jacob, but he trusted that Karma could hold her own with him.

Duke ducked behind a pile of rubble.

It was too dark in the alley for Ridge to discern what the pile was made of. He waited.

Allie reached the lowest tier of the fire escape, about fifteen feet off the ground, and her eyes met Ridge's. She stepped back, likely alerted by the direct eye contact that he *knew* they were there. She made a couple of gestures with her hands, then pointed at Ridge. She released the ladder.

The loud screeching as the ladder descended echoed through the alley. Duke stepped out from behind the rubble pile, absently tossing a large shard of brick in his hand.

"Again, really?" Ridge asked, tipping his head at the brick.

Meg carried a hunk of rebar.

Malcolm still peeked around the corner, not venturing into the alley itself, but watching the others.

Ridge heard noise behind him, where Karma and Jacob were. He stepped to the side, blocking the door with his body. He wasn't afraid Jacob could do him any harm, and he'd shield Karma if it were her coming behind him.

Duke came at him first.

Ridge clocked the fist swinging his way and ducked. He reached out, grabbing the rebar being swung at him with his left hand. The sting in his palm from the speed and strength with which the rebar hit made him growl.

Allie attempted to drive her shoulder into Ridge's gut.

Ridge shifted his weight and swiveled his hips.

Her shoulder clipped Ridge's hip bone hard enough to leave a mark, but she sailed right past him.

Catching her backside with his boot, Ridge shoved her headfirst into the wall behind him.

Meg caught Ridge with a punch to his nose.

His vision blurred as his eyes teared up from the impact and sting.

The big man roared, pulling Ridge's attention, and a shrill whistle set his ears to ringing, the piercing noise nearly bringing him to his knees.

The rebar locked around his throat, and a large knee pressed into his back. He struggled to pull air as he worked to get his hands between the rebar and his neck. Meg hung on his back, refusing to give an inch.

Air swirled against the side of his face as a fist sailed past his ear, a foot propped on his half-bent leg to add height to the assailant. The rebar tightened against his neck for an instant before it fell away.

He turned his attention behind him to find Meg flat on her back, disoriented.

The scrape of the rebar being lifted from the ground made him turn back to the scrum.

Karma held the rebar over her shoulder like a baseball bat, about to swing it at Duke.

The shrill whistle sounded again, louder this time, and the big man dropped to his knees.

The swing of the rebar caused its own whistle as it sailed over the head of the big guy with blinding speed, clanging loudly against the nearest dumpster, drowning out the dreaded whistle for a second.

Karma's scent surrounded him as she backed into Ridge, pushing him against the wall, shielding him. Her ears weren't as sensitive to that shrill whistle, and she adjusted her hold on the rebar, readying another strike.

The next "bong" rang out, and the whistle, thankfully, cut off.

Chapter 18

5713

Karma

The rancid smell of the alley gave her a headache, and she wanted out of there as soon as possible. Ridge had blood running from his nose, where it looked like it had been broken.

This little sojourn was taking up too much time. She wanted to be back at their place with the kids by first light. It didn't look like they were going to make it, this trip, to the sewer entrance of Phoenix Corps she'd used when rescuing Lily to see if there were any changes there.

Her patience was shot between dealing with Jacob and now this guy and his minions. "Just the asshole I was looking for. Malcolm." She nodded in greeting.

"We need to talk to you. Alone."

"I've already told you. You get both of us or none of us. If you want my help, you will include Ridge."

"You said you didn't have strength anymore. This little demonstration,"—he waved his hand—"proves otherwise."

"Whatever they gave me is finally getting out of my system, apparently. I'm still not at a hundred percent. I won't go in without Ridge."

"Fine, but we aren't discussing this here." Malcolm turned on his heel and walked out of the alley the way he'd come. His minions followed.

Karma didn't move.

Ridge stayed at her side.

A minute later, his bony shoulders reappeared at the edge of the alleyway. "Coming?"

Karma kept her feet planted. "We can talk here."

"Look," he started, annoyance evident in his tone.

"Are we really going to do this again?" Karma pointed the rebar at him. "You cornered him and attacked. I don't know you from Adam. I certainly don't trust you. You want me to blindly follow you? Fat chance."

"You think you have a choice in the matter?"

His minions reappeared at the edge of the alley.

Karma huffed. "You can try them again. At least one of them is in no condition to continue to fight. I don't like your odds. But it's your bet to take."

"Then where?"

She turned and shouldered her way into the room she was just in, pulling Ridge behind her. She kept the rebar in her hand. Once inside, she gathered a clean piece of gauze from Jacob's first aid kit and sat Ridge in a chair at the table, then proceeded to clean up the blood from his face, ignoring Jacob's sulking and the others entering the small room.

Karma cleaned up the blood and checked over Ridge for other injuries. The bruising along his throat made her blood boil. "Someone saw us as we headed to Finley Avenue. They apparently ran to tell that one." Karma pointed at Malcolm. "He then sent Jacob into our path to catch my attention." She stood, turning her attention to him. "I get that no one around here is friendly anymore. Everyone sticks to themselves as much as possible, because it is dangerous to do anything else. Jacob could have told you that I am not like most. I've helped as many people as I could since the quake, especially since I escaped Phoenix Corps."

"We don't need him." Malcolm's frustration was clear as he paced in the small space, shouldering his minions out of the way as he passed them.

"If you want *me*, you get him, too."

Malcolm spun on his heel and stopped, glaring at Ridge. "I don't trust him."

"I don't trust you." Karma casually sat back down next to Ridge, laying her hand on his thigh. "I guess we are at an impasse." She turned to Ridge. "Feeling up to the walk home?"

He nodded, and they headed for the door.

"Wait!" Malcolm cried out. "Fine. Have it your way." His shoulders slumped, and he pouted like a toddler.

They slowly retook their seats, and Karma placed her elbows on the table, resting her chin in her hands. "What is in these files? And what do you want from *us*?"

"On the upper floors of the facility is where the pencil pushers, as you called me, work. I worked in acquisitions to coordinate the exchange of information with other facilities about their experiments. Not only that, I was tasked with identifying outside companies that were conducting similar tests, acquiring their records, and/or recruiting their employees for our staff. With the access I had, I managed to find out that not only is Phoenix Corps supplying their Altereds to our government, but they have shopped around their services to foreign governments."

"They are telling other governments how to create their own super soldiers?" Ridge asked.

"No. Andrew Phoenix isn't stupid. He wants the monopoly on where these governments can acquire their super soldiers. He doesn't want them to be able to make them themselves."

"Then he's not very smart, because I'm pretty sure another government could reverse engineer what Phoenix Corps is doing and figure it out themselves," Karma replied.

"The trackers Phoenix Corps puts in their Altereds aren't just for locating the soldiers. They've used nanotechnology to hardwire the trackers into the nervous system. They aren't so easy to just cut out as the ones you and *he* were given. Those little trackers have switches that can be flipped, creating the ability to control the Altered from afar. Phoenix can turn those soldiers into assassins if he so chooses. He can also recall them to him and virtually 'download' the information those soldiers have gathered on the foreign nation and their plans. They are automatically set to fundamentally alter the blood of the soldiers, so any attempt to copy or reproduce their results is nearly impossible. And none of these countries know of these aspects.

"And their *human* experiments aren't the only thing Phoenix is up to. Some of the numbers weren't adding up. That's what had me searching their records, squirreling away information to use later. About ten years ago, there was an obscene amount of money being filtered into a research and development team. References were made in the records about some sort of satellite technology. I didn't understand all of it, but abruptly, the money being funneled there was cut off."

"You have information on all of this? Proof?"

"Yes. I have it hidden inside the facility, and I need to get in and get it."

"Why didn't you bring it out with you? If it was so important, why did you leave it behind?" Karma asked.

"Someone must have noticed something. They assigned guards to me, and rarely did I have a moment alone. I snuck away from my guards on my way back from a walk. I managed to find a break in the fence and escape while they were distracted, probably from one of your many visits," he looked at Karma. "You did like to cause a stir."

Ridge leaned forward. "What makes you think those records are still hidden for you to retrieve?"

"If they found out I kept and hid copies of those records, I'd have been disposed of long before I could escape. And I'm not stupid. I hid it where they wouldn't look, even if they had a reason to search. I never gave them any indication that I was planning to escape or that I was squirreling away information to use against them."

"Who do you plan to give the files to?" she asked.

"Media. Government officials who aren't in Phoenix's pocket."

"Media? There's still media out there?"

"There's a whole functioning world out there."

Karma gasped.

"The areas Pheonix Corps has 'helped' are isolated on purpose. They can't have you reaching out to people you know who live in other parts of the country. If this kind of experimenting and treatment got out to the general public, the government would have an uprising on its hands."

"How far away are the nearest habitable areas?"

"A lot of people were brought into Meridian, the main capital. That's where Phoenix recruited me from."

"Meridian? That's five hundred miles away!" Ridge's wide eyes met hers.

"There's nothing between here and there?" Karma asked.

"A few minor towns are building up again. But people were scared after the disasters and ran to the nearest big city. Unfortunately for you, the closest large city on this side of Meridian was Fairway."

"Why did you escape from your cushy job at Phoenix Corps? Why are you trying to take them down, now?"

"I suspected they wanted me gone. I hacked into one of the systems and I was next up to be Altered. I don't want to be made into a freak."

Karma glanced at Ridge. He and a couple of the others stiffened at the declaration.

"Not wanting to be Altered, I get that. Calling us 'freaks'? I'd be careful what you say with the company you keep."

"Would you allow them to alter you, knowing what you know now?" His sneer as he spoke was filled with disdain.

"No. But am I a freak? Also no. And, if I weren't a 'freak,' I probably wouldn't be of use to you, now would I?"

Malcolm's jaw tightened in agitation. But he couldn't dispute her argument.

Ridge steered them back on track. "Where is it hidden?"

Malcolm scoffed. "Why would I tell you that?"

"Umm, because you want us to go get it for you." Ridge raised his eyebrow.

"I didn't say that. I'll get the records. You get me in."

Karma looked at Ridge and back. She couldn't hide the disbelief in her voice. "You want me to take you into the facility so you can get these records?"

"Yes."

"And when you get caught?"

"You won't let me get caught."

Karma raised her eyebrows at his statement but didn't respond. "What floor are your records on?"

"The seventh."

Karma laughed. "I've never been above the second floor. I have no idea where anything is or what security measures are in place."

"I still have my access card. I can get in."

"And you think your access card is still active? The moment you disappeared, they pulled your access," Ridge countered.

Malcolm must not have thought about that, because his smug expression sobered.

"Why is it so important for you to get these records?" Ridge asked. Karma heard the wariness in his voice, but she didn't think the others caught it.

"I don't like what they are doing to people."

"They've been torturing us for over ten years now. And *now*, you decide something needs to be done? What changed? Is it just because your ass was about to be in the sling?"

"You don't have to believe my motives. I don't care. But I need you, Karma, to get me inside so I can get the records and turn them over."

"I don't know the upper floors. Even if I did, the risk of getting caught is so much higher when bringing in someone untrained. Hell, they caught me when

I was alone. I don't know why you think I can get you in and out without getting caught. Let alone the fact that it's in a part of the building I've never been in before. I'm not a miracle worker; I can't walk through locked doors or walls without breaking through or setting off an alarm. I can't make myself invisible from their security cameras."

"You've gotten in and out dozens of times, according to Jacob. Surely, you can handle this." Desperation filled his tone. "The information in there could shut down Phoenix Corps permanently. Either by our government or others, once they know he's playing both sides and keeping information from them."

Chapter 19

Ridge

"What kind of fairy tale are you living in that you thought tattling to the government, *any government*, would result in them coming in and shutting down their super soldier supplier? Do you think they will be any better? According to you, these governments are knowingly *buying* victims of Phoenix Corps experiments. Who says they stand on any sort of moral high ground when it comes to this?"

"Phoenix Corps is more powerful than you know," Malcolm shouted. "They have more influence than you can believe, and they are amassing more and more of it every day. The longer it goes on, the more powerful they will be."

Karma pounded her fist on the rickety table, eliciting an ominous cracking sound, but it held. "And how do you expect the few people standing here right now to change that?"

"If we alert the government with proof, they have the power to stop him."

"Do they?" Ridge asked. He stood and paced the few steps available on his side of the table. He stopped behind Karma, placing his hands on her shoulders. "Pip told Karma that Phoenix has influence over the government. Who's to say that they will lift a finger to stop what Phoenix Corps is doing to the people here?"

"There's more than one Phoenix Corps out there," Malcolm said. "This isn't the only place they are running their experiments."

"If that's true, then even if we can do something to stop *this* facility, what difference does it make?" Karma hung her head. "If nowhere is safe..."

"Do you have a plan?" Ridge asked.

"Yeah. Karma gets us in and up to the seventh floor. I retrieve the files, and she gets us back out."

Karma rolled her eyes. "While that sounds like a spectacular plan, what happens when we run into the goon squad? When we find the doors locked? When we get cornered and can't get out?"

"Allie can blow a hole in almost anything with the explosives she has access to. If we get stuck somewhere, she can get us through. Meg can pick or break locks. Duke's been known to talk himself out of a plethora of bad situations, and I'm the only one who knows the location of the files. And Jacob knows tech. He might be able to disable some of their systems. I've got the tools," he waved his hand to indicate the others in the room. "I just need the map." He pointed at her.

"Whoa, whoa, whoa," Karma said, holding up her hands. "You expect me to get *all* of you into the building unnoticed? You have got to be joking!"

"I don't trust you any more than you trust me. I'm not giving you the location of the files, and I'm certainly not going in there without someone I know will watch my back."

"Jacob, why would you ever want to go back in there?"

His eyes slid to Allie, then back to Karma, and held steady. "I worked for *them*. I helped design some of their security systems. While I have no doubt they've updated and improved some of those systems, there's a good possibility that I can still crack into the programs or bypass systems."

Ridge pulled her to her feet and wrapped an arm around her. He turned his head to meet Malcolm's eyes. "We'll come back tomorrow with an answer."

"I need an answer now!" he demanded.

Ridge looked pointedly at each of Malcolm's personal goon squad members before coming to rest on Malcolm once more. "The answer, right this moment, is no. If you want a chance at a different answer, you will wait until tomorrow. Follow us, and you'll regret it." He led Karma past the others and into the alley. They didn't stop until they were just a few minutes from home.

Ridge pulled her into a small copse of trees. "Let's wait here a few minutes, make sure we weren't followed. I don't think we were, but better safe than sorry."

She nodded absently and searched the area with her eyes. Karma sighed when he stepped up behind her, wrapping his arms around her middle.

"You're cold." He pulled her shivering form tighter to him, sharing his warmth.

"What happens if we leave here with the kids, and out there is more dangerous?"

"We'll figure out how to keep them safe out there, just like you learned here."

They stood in silence, watching for any movement, until the dark haze of the night faded into the lighter haze of the day.

Karma broke the silence with a whisper. "What do we do?"

Ridge turned her in his arms, taking her lips in a kiss he hoped conveyed the love he felt but didn't have the words to describe. He was out of breath when he pulled away. "If anyone can get in and out of Phoenix Corps, it's you. But this trip will be fraught with much more danger than ever before. You are going in blind. That doesn't even account for the fact that you'd be taking an unknown group of people inside and trusting that it's not some sort of elaborate trap."

"I don't even know where to begin to mitigate any of the danger." Karma snuggled tighter into his arms, burying her face against his shoulder. Her vulnerability pulled at his heart, making him want to take on the world for her. "If we get caught in there, if we can't get out, what happens to the kids?"

"Until my last breath, I won't stop fighting to get us out of there," he vowed. "But in the event that we can't get to them, Lily is tough and smart, just like you. Peter is learning quickly. Together, they can make it."

The dampness he felt through his shirt from her silent tears broke his heart. He held her while she cried silently, running his hands over her arms and back for comfort and warmth.

When she pulled away, her eyes were puffy and red. "I'm sorry."

"Nothing to be sorry for," Ridge replied, wiping the last of the tears from her cheeks. "You've been through a lot these last few months, without adding the decade before that. It's enough to break any-one."

Ridge turned his head sharply at a whisper of sound.

Lily stood about twenty feet away.

"What happened? Is Karma ok?"

Karma stiffened and shifted to face her. "I thought we told you to stay in the basement."

"You were gone all night," Lily said. "I planned to check the traps and see if I could find you, if you were nearby." Lily kicked at a stone. "I told Peter to stay inside."

"You should stick together. If Karma or I aren't around, you are responsible for keeping both of you safe."

Lily lowered her eyes and kicked at the ground again.

"Come on," Karma said, throwing her arm over Lily's shoulders. "Let's go check the traps."

If he hadn't been standing there a few moments ago, he'd have believed the light-hearted tone Karma used.

Peter had been pacing at the bottom of the stairs by the time they returned with a rabbit from one of their traps. He dove into Karma's arms the moment her feet hit the floor, hugging her tightly.

Karma kept things upbeat and fun, teasing the kids and playing games while they made short work of breakfast. It all came to a halt once the kitchen was clean.

"Get an extra layer of clothes on, we are going for a walk," Karma said to the kids.

Ridge walked up behind her, placing his hands on her hips. "What are you thinking?"

Karma turned in his arms and raised her eyes to his. "We walk to the path Lily and I took... wow, was that just yesterday? Anyway, we go to the gap I found in the fissure that isn't too big to cross. We can scavenge some boards from the nearby structures and make a makeshift bridge. If we don't make it back, the kids still have a way to leave." Her voice cracked on the last words, and tears filled her eyes, but didn't fall.

"So, we are going in?"

"You don't have to..."

"If you go, I go. We're a package deal, remember?" He winked at her as he tossed her words back at her.

Relief washed over her face. "Thank you."

"There's never been another option." Ridge dropped a kiss on the end of her nose as Lily and Peter emerged from their rooms.

A smile back on her face, but not quite reaching her eyes, she said, "Lily, you take the lead." Karma swept her arm in front of her and waited until both Lily and Peter passed before falling into line behind them.

Ridge took up the rear, closing the bulkhead doors behind him and keeping a close watch of their surroundings as they moved through the trees. He smiled to himself, proud that neither Lily nor Peter needed a reminder. They moved silently through the trees, careful of where they stepped and what they brushed against, to hide their trail as best they could. Both kids listened and learned fast. He'd do whatever it took to make sure Karma made it back to them. But if he failed, they'd still be alright.

Chapter 20

5713

Karma

Karma's mind spun as she followed Lily and Peter into the woods and beyond. At the edge of the trees, the fissure marred the landscape in front of them. The possibilities of what lay past the horizon were endless. Paradise could be waiting for them, safety, security... hell, there could be easy access to food again. But the opposite was also a possibility. More hardship, more danger, and all of it unknown.

Peter tripped on unexpectedly uneven ground, and Karma's arm shot out to steady him. If she wasn't with them when they left, who would catch him? Who would keep them safe? They were capable, yes.

But they were just kids. They shouldn't have to fend for themselves.

Tears welled up in her eyes again, and Karma blinked them away.

As if sensing her distress, Ridge closed the distance between them, resting his hand on the small of her back. That small connection eased the vise constricting her lungs, and she pulled in a steadying breath.

In front, Lily stopped and held up her hand. Everyone stopped behind her, then the group eased back into the trees.

A rabbit darted out from the trees, halted, and turned its head, then scampered back into the brush.

"Good job, Lily," Ridge praised.

Lily stepped back out of the tree line and continued to lead, with Peter not far behind.

Ridge held Karma back, allowing the kids to get out of hearing range. "Whatever happens, they'll be fine."

Unable to speak around the emotions clogging her throat, Karma dipped her head in affirmation.

About an hour later, they finally made it to the smaller gap in the fissure.

Ridge leapt over the gap, testing the stability on the other side. "The fissure isn't as deep here, but some of those rocks look razor sharp. It'd be difficult to navigate. With the kids and supplies, a bridge will be the best bet." He returned to their side of the fissure and looked at the remains of the buildings. "Let's start in this one and work our way around."

Peter followed at Ridge's heels, but Lily stayed with Karma.

"What's going on?" Lily asked, as she yanked at a piece of drywall, dampened from exposure.

"What do you mean?" Karma busied herself on the neighboring wall, inspecting any boards long enough to serve her purpose.

Lily cocked her hip and gave Karma an incredulous look. "I'm not stupid. Something happened last night."

She stopped and turned to face Lily, giving her Karma's full attention. "You are far from stupid." She sat on the floor and patted the spot next to her. Karma fought to keep her emotions contained as she met Lily's eyes. "I've got to get back into Phoenix Corps one more time." Holding up her hand to stave off the protest, she continued, "We need to get some proof of what they are doing. I don't know who can stop Phoenix Corps, but someone has to."

"Can't someone else go? You've been in and out so many times. And last time…"

"Trust me, if there were someone else I could send, I would. That's the last thing I *want* to do."

"Is Ridge going, too?"

"Yes," Ridge answered, coming around the wall with his hand on Peter's shoulder.

"Can we help?" Peter asked, his hero worship for Ridge glowing in his eyes.

"You can help us by watching out for each other while we are gone," Karma answered. She turned her gaze back to Lily. "You found your way back here. You know how to listen to your surroundings and keep yourself and Peter safe."

"No!" she protested.

Karma took Lily's hand. "We're planning on coming back. We aren't leaving you. But you need to be prepared in case something happens and we can't get back. When we go to Phoenix Corps, you will wait one day for us. If we aren't back, you get Peter and supplies, and you come here. Get yourself and Peter across the fissure and head west."

Tears ran down Lily's face, and Peter buried his face in Ridge's shoulder.

"If we're just delayed, we will catch up to you. If not, you go as far as you can, as fast as you can."

Lily shook her head with every word.

"Lily, I can't go unless I know you will do what I ask. If I'm worried about you, I can't fully concentrate on the task in front of me. I need to know that you will keep yourself and Peter safe if I can't be there."

"I won't stop fighting until Karma is home with you, Lily. I promise you that," Ridge vowed.

Karma lifted her eyes to his. If he thought for one moment she'd allow him to sacrifice himself to get her out, he had a lesson to learn. But she didn't speak, noticing that his declaration eased some of the tension Lily had been holding. Instead, she stood, brushing her hands off on her jeans and reaching out a hand to help Lily up.

Once on her feet, Lily wrapped her arms around Karma, holding on for all she was worth. Peter's weight slammed into them a moment later, joining their fierce hug. Ridge's hand came to rest on her shoulder, giving her a reassuring squeeze, which was the only thing to keep the tears at bay. It didn't matter that she hadn't birthed these children. They were hers. The thought that they might be on their own, fending for themselves in a matter of days, terrified her.

Lily pulled away first and straightened to her full height. She cleared her throat and spun on her heel, returning to the wall and tearing down another chunk of limp drywall.

Pride tried to choke her.

Lily had been a spunky and rebellious kid when Karma met her. She'd lost her childhood to this horrid place, but that young woman wouldn't let anything keep her down for long. Even if they didn't make it back, Lily would be okay, and she would make sure Peter was well cared for.

Karma forced her gaze away from Lily before she fell completely apart again and tore at her own wall.

By the time they were all finished, they'd amassed a good number of pieces of lumber they could use. They dragged the pieces to the fissure and, using some of the old nails they salvaged, Karma and Ridge taught the kids to build a sturdy bridge that would span the fissure and carry them away from Fairway.

Chapter 21

Ridge

Ridge quietly lifted Karma and placed her in their bed. He backed out of the room and stopped next to the table. "I'll be back in a few hours."

"Where are you going?" Lily asked slowly.

"Just to talk to the people who asked for our help."

"Karma won't like you going close to Phoenix Corps without her," Peter piped up.

"I'm not going in without her."

"If she has to come save your ass, she'll kick it after."

Ridge couldn't help but laugh. "I'll tell Karma you said so."

Peter's eyes grew three sizes, and Lily chuckled.

"I won't be gone too long. I want to get a timeframe for when they want to move on the building. Karma needs to rest."

"Be careful," Lily murmured as he headed for the door.

"Stay inside. Get some rest yourselves." With that, Ridge moved up the stairs, closing the bulkhead doors behind him.

Staying in the deepening shadows, Ridge moved from building to building, making his way back to Finley Avenue. He was only a block away from the trailer park when he heard voices.

He scurried into the remnants of a brick building and worked his way over to the back corner. The bricks muffled the sounds, but he could still make out two distinct voices. Ridge ground his teeth together as he recognized one of the voices, Annabeth.

"She wouldn't just disappear! She's hiding in the city somewhere. You need to get your head out of your ass and *find* her!" Annabeth was screeching.

"We're clearing the city block by block. There's been no sign. And, you said they took away her animal. She's no longer a threat." The deep baritone of the other voice wasn't one Ridge was familiar with.

"She's a threat as long as she's alive. That bitch doesn't know when to quit."

Ridge clamped his fists tighter. He wanted to rip Annabeth apart, both for her deception, which had been the catalyst for Karma's capture by Pip and the Phoenix Corps after all the help she had given to Annabeth over the years, and for the way she was speaking about her now.

"I think she might be dead. You said the serum they gave her could be enough to kill her."

The sound of flesh cracking against flesh echoed against the bricks.

"No one gave you permission to think!" Madness rode her voice. "I'll arrange for more teams to start searching. Send some teams back into the areas that have already been cleared. I don't want anywhere left for her to hide in. Go into Finley Avenue first thing tomorrow. We'll start tearing shit apart in there."

"Finley?" the baritone of his voice cracked, jumping several octaves.

"Grow a pair, Gruff. I said Finley. You go to fucking Finley!"

Gruff grunted as a dull thud reached Ridge's ears, followed by a strained gasp for air—a punch to the solar plexus, if Ridge had to guess.

Ridge held perfectly still, not daring to do much more than breathe as he waited for Annabeth and her punching bag to move on to a different area. When the coast was clear, he picked up his pace and moved in the shadows, ears peeled for any hint that he was near other goon squad members.

Once he reached the Finley Avenue area, Ridge made a beeline for Jacob's place from the night before. All the smells surrounding the alley were old. He knocked on the door several times but got no response. Ridge put his shoulder into the not-so-sturdy door and shoved his way inside.

With all that had gone on the night before, Ridge hadn't registered until this moment that Jacob's scent hadn't been more prominent in here than anyone else's. This might have been where Jacob brought them, but this wasn't where he lived. He let out a frustrated growl and moved back into the alleyway. Of course, they couldn't make it easy for him to find them.

The stench of the alleyway messed with his ability to sort through the scents, so he walked to the opposite end from where he entered. The first scent he caught was the woman who'd tried to choke him with rebar, Meg. He zeroed in on her smell and followed his nose deeper into the Finley Avenue neighborhood.

The skin along his back prickled with warning as he moved further in, sensing the eyes of others watching his every move and step. Ridge knew there weren't any Phoenix Corp goons around yet, so he wasn't sneaking around; he was plainly walking down the center of the street, hoping that one of Malcolm's people would get word to him that Ridge was here. It didn't take long.

Ridge slowed his steps as he approached the end of a block. The cross street was just as dark as the one he was on, but something in his gut sent out a warning.

Meg crept out of the shadows at his slowed pace and tapped another piece of rebar on the palm of her hand.

"Glad you see you are back on your feet," Ridge said casually.

"You don't belong here."

"I need to talk to Malcolm."

"You don't belong here."

"Not hard of hearing. I heard you the first time. Doesn't change the facts."

"You…"

"Skip to the next track, please." Ridge shook off his annoyance. "Malcolm didn't exactly leave a callback number, and wherever Jacob lured us to isn't where he 'lives,' so I came here to give Malcolm our answer and some information I've come across. It would be helpful if you could get him. Or take me to him."

She huffed and spun away, shouting "Stay where you are!" over her shoulder as she disappeared back down the way she'd come.

He fought the urge to shift uncomfortably as he waited, still feeling so many eyes on him, but he stayed where he was. An eternity seemed to pass before the woman reappeared and beckoned him closer. The piece of rebar still in her hand, she swung it absently, glancing over her shoulder periodically to make sure he was following.

"Wait here." She pointed with the rebar to a long-abandoned car. Rust spots stained the ground from the rain running off the rusted-out body, and all the windows were shattered; the insides had been stripped down to the bare metal.

Ridge leaned his hip against the rough texture of the once smooth frame and waited. Waiting again, he picked out the familiar smells that were stronger here. Malcolm and the four others had to be in this area fairly frequently for their scents to be this strong. He caught the subtly sweet smell Karma had followed the night before, recognizing it as Jacob's. His ears picked up footsteps coming from his right. Adjusting only his eyes, he caught a glimpse of the woman again, along with her friends. She'd disappeared to his left, and he hadn't heard other movement, so he assumed she had crossed his path underground somehow.

That godawful whistling noise came from his left, but he stood stock still until Malcolm came into view. Jacob trailed behind.

"You don't belong here."

"Yeah, I heard that somewhere before." Ridge shoved off the car to his full height. "I came to talk to you. You don't want the information? I'll happily leave you to your fate."

"Where's Karma?"

"Resting."

"I told you both, I'm looking for *her* help. Not yours. I'm not following you into Phoenix Corps."

"I'm not going into Phoenix Corps without her. She has discovered more ways in and out of that place than I can count. It would be suicide to go in there blind without her."

"Then why are you here?"

"I came here because we've agreed to help you."

"You've passed on the information. Come back with Karma, and we can discuss it further."

"Finding you has been a problem, so I need to know a better way to do it. I also happened near some talking goon squad idiots on my way here. They are talking about coming to Finley Avenue tomorrow morning. I figured you would want to know, so you can scatter and keep your people safe."

"Phoenix Corps doesn't come to Finley."

"Maybe not before, but I very clearly heard them say they are coming here tomorrow," Ridge countered.

"Why would they come here now?"

"According to the conversation I heard, they are pissed off that they can't find Karma. They are doubling back on some of the areas they've already searched, probably thinking we would assume already searched areas would be safe. Annabeth betrayed Karma. She's the reason Phoenix Corps got their hands on her the last time. She seems to be running the goon squad searches. She ordered them to start on Finley Avenue tomorrow. I know you aren't the only ones here. If any of you value your safety and freedom, you need to get out of Finley fast."

"They won't find us." Malcolm's cockiness set Ridge's teeth on edge.

"Don't be so sure."

Jacob surprised Ridge by speaking up. "Annabeth is vicious when she wants to be. And she won't back down. If she thinks Karma is here, she'll tear this place apart to find her. Above and *below* ground."

Ridge turned away and headed back the way he came. "I'm leaving. Do what you want. I'll bring Karma to the trailer park tomorrow night. Leave a sign somewhere near what's left of Jacob's trailer, and we'll come meet you to discuss the plan for getting back into Phoenix Corps, if you're still around."

Chapter 22

Karma

The bed dipped beside her, and Karma opened her eyes. The darkness of the room kept her from seeing any details, except Ridge's outline as he climbed in. His skin was cold, even to her touch, when she reached out to him. "Why are you so cold?"

"I just got back from visiting Malcolm. I'll tell you about it in the morning. Go back to sleep, baby." Ridge pulled the covers over himself and wrapped her in his chilly embrace.

She snuggled in close. "Why did you go without me?"

"You needed rest. We both need rest now. Tomorrow, I'll fill you in."

The grogginess in his voice was evident, and her eyes were still heavy. "You're in the doghouse for going without me. But that can wait until we've both had more sleep." Karma yawned and buried herself against his rapidly warming skin, basking in the heat.

His lips pressed into her forehead as she drifted back to sleep.

Ridge still slept as light filtered in through the small window in the bedroom.

Sounds of the kids making breakfast reached her ears. Karma crept out of bed and went out to help. Curiosity burned at her, remembering the snippet of their conversation when Ridge crawled into bed the night before, but he needed sleep, so she'd keep herself busy until he woke.

The chill of the basement seeped into her bones. She missed the underground tunnel and room she'd made in the trailer park. It maintained a constant temperature, regardless of the heat or chill of the weather above ground. Winter was fast approaching, and even if they could stay here, it wouldn't work.

Quietly closing the bedroom door behind her, Karma stood and observed the children.

Lily and Peter joked around as they worked companionably in the kitchen. Peter washed something in the sink while Lily cooked at the stove. He splashed her with some water, making her jump and squeal. He doubled over in laughter until she dumped a can of water on his head while he was distracted. Peter gasped and grabbed more water to retaliate. Lily noticed Karma and stopped in her tracks, her eyes wide with surprise. They widened further when Peter dumped one last can of water down Lily's back.

Karma couldn't help but laugh. "Okay, you two. Get dry clothes on. It's too cold in here for you to be walking around like that. I'll finish breakfast. You can help clean up your mess when you are dry."

Working on autopilot, Karma finished preparing breakfast, her mind on the dangers ahead.

"I think that spot is clean," Ridge said, placing his hands on her shoulders, pressing into her back.

The kids stood off to the side of the kitchen, watching her, worry etched into their features.

Ridge laid one of his hands over hers, the one holding the rag, and gently pried it out of her white-knuckle grip.

She blinked, her brain coming back to the present, and turned to Ridge.

"Go ahead and eat, kids. We'll be back in a few minutes." Ridge led her into their bedroom, her hand still engulfed in his, and shut the door behind them. He sat on the edge of the bed and waited until she took her place next to him before speaking again. "You okay?"

She nodded. "Why did you go without me last night? What happened?"

"Hang on a second. We'll get to that. Where were you just now?"

Karma took a deep breath. "Just thinking about everything. All the unknowns are overwhelming. I walked out there this morning, and the kids were having fun, acting like kids should. I want more of that for them. And if something happens to us, if they are left on their own..."

Ridge gathered her to him, his arms secure and comforting. She felt less alone now, here, with him, in his arms, and it scared her. Growing accustomed to the security he provided, she was no longer so alone. The thought of losing it, losing him, being all on her own again, was terrifying. She soaked in his warmth and love, surrounding herself with the much-needed peace that insulated her from the turbulent thoughts plaguing her.

After a few minutes, she pulled away to look at him. "Tell me why you went without me last night."

"You hadn't slept." He raised his hand to stop her when she would have argued that he hadn't slept either. "You're still recovering, and we needed to give Malcolm our answer. Anyway, it's a good thing I went when I did. I ran into Annabeth and one of her goons."

Karma's blood boiled with rage, and she started checking him for injuries.

"They didn't see me, but I could hear them," he assured her. Ridge explained what he had heard and told her about going to Finley Avenue and meeting with Malcolm. "We'll go together to the trailer park tonight to find his message, then go from there."

"We should prepare the kids for tonight. Make sure they have everything packed and ready to go, so they can leave if..." Her voice cracked as her emotion threatened to choke her.

"I'll make sure you get home to them, Karma. No matter what."

Karma laid her hand on his cheek, drawing him closer. "I need you to come home with me," she pleaded. She sealed her mouth over his, pouring into the kiss her love and her fears.

Panting hard, he dropped his forehead to hers as the kiss ended. "I'm going to fight like hell to get both of us out of there." He'd slid his hand beneath the hem of her shirt during their kiss, and his thumb drifted over the sensitive skin beneath her ribs.

She curled into him, breathing in the peace, love, and contentment he offered. For just a moment, she could bask in him, before they walked out the door and into the very heart of the fear that drove her.

Not enough time passed before she stood, her hand entwined with his, unable to let go. Karma led the way out of the bedroom, forcing herself not to look longingly at the room she was leaving behind.

Lily and Peter followed her with their eyes as she took her place at the table.

Ridge stood behind her, still holding her hand, his free hand on her shoulder.

"I'm going to help you pack supplies and clothes. We are going to meet up with the people who want our help getting into Phoenix Corps. One more night here, that's what you get. If we aren't back by the time you finish breakfast, I want you on the bridge and out of Fairway."

"But…" Lily started.

"No buts. Head west, and do not look back. If we are just delayed, we *will* catch up with you. If not, do not come back here. Do not look for us. You know how to take care of each other." Karma bit the inside of her cheek to fight off the tears determined to fall. "Find shelter. Trap food. Grow food. Whatever you do, stay out of Phoenix Corps' grasp."

"But we don't know what's out there," Peter protested.

"No, we don't. But we know what's here. We know the danger Phoenix Corps poses. They will find us here eventually. It is quickly growing cold. Too cold for us to stay in this basement, anyway. As nice as this is, we'd never be able to stay here through the winter."

"You could build us another tunnel," Lily chimed in. "It was almost always the same temperature in the tunnel. We wintered there every year."

"I don't have the time, and with Phoenix Corps doing sweeps, they'll find us sooner or later. I won't take the chance that they get their hands on either of you."

"But, if you and Ridge destroy Phoenix Corps when you go back there, won't it be safe for us here then?" Peter asked.

Karma shook her head sadly. "I'm not going in there with the intent to kill everyone, Peter. I don't know that just Ridge and I *could* destroy the building. The most important thing I can do is to keep you and Lily safe. And, right now, the safest place for you is away from Fairway."

When Peter opened his mouth to voice another argument, Ridge cleared his throat, stopping Peter before he got started.

"I'll help Peter pack," Ridge said, motioning to Peter to follow him into the room with the bunk beds he'd claimed.

Karma stood, leading Lily into the room she'd chosen.

Lily followed, slamming the door shut behind her. "There has to be another way!" she shouted.

Karma sat on the edge of the bed and patted the spot next to her.

Lily paced in front of her, refusing to sit.

"Phoenix Corps has to be stopped," Karma said softly.

Lily's shoulders sagged. "But why does it have to be you?"

"Because I can. If I stop them, *you* are safer. Peter is safer. The rest of the world can go to hell, but for you and Peter, I'll do whatever it takes to keep you safe."

"But if we leave…"

"We don't know how far their reach goes. As long as Phoenix Corps exists, we'll never be truly safe."

Tears fell freely down Lily's cheeks. "What if you don't make it back, if I'm all that's left to take care of Peter?"

Karma grasped Lily's hands, pulling her to a stop, and waited until their eyes met. "You've been helping me to keep Peter safe for years. And now, he's old enough to help. I have no doubt that you can keep him safe. But Lily, I won't ever stop fighting to get back to you, okay?"

Lily nodded sadly.

Wrapping Lily in her arms, Karma held her until the tears subsided. Before releasing her hold, Karma uttered, "You've got this, Lily. I am so proud of you."

Lily gave her a watery smile and picked up the pack she would use to carry supplies.

Chapter 23

Karma

Karma found Peter and Ridge sitting on the couch, heads bowed and whispering animatedly.

She set Lily's pack on the floor next to Peter's. "Ridge and I will be leaving soon. Make sure you eat well today, and before you set out tomorrow. If we aren't back yet, start early. Get as far west as you can, as quickly as you can. We'll find you as soon as we are able."

"We've got this, Karma." Confidence rode Peter's tone as he stood up and, of all things, saluted her.

She ruffled the hair on his head and walked past, entering the room she shared with Ridge, and started filling a pack for herself.

His footsteps followed her into the room, and he worked on loading his own supplies. "They'll be fine, Karma."

Unable to trust her voice, she just nodded, kept her head down, and shoved additional clothes into her pack. Once complete, she pushed her pack into the corner of the room, next to the one Ridge had just finished. "Ready?"

He pulled her in, wrapping her in his arms and allowing her to forget for a moment the danger they faced, as his lips claimed hers in a passionate kiss.

"We'll come back for the packs when we are done helping Malcolm," Karma said when she pulled away.

Ridge led her from the room.

"We're heading out," Karma said, drawing each of the kids into a tight hug. "Remember, eat…"

"Eat well. Be gone early tomorrow. You'll catch up. I know," Lily parroted back to her. "We've got it. I won't let you down."

Karma tightened her arms around Lily once more. "You could never let me down, Lily. I'm so proud of you."

"Get going." Lily pushed her toward the door. "The sooner you get there, the sooner you come back. We should all head out together."

"Don't wait for us. We'll find you if we get delayed."

"I know." Lily's tone betrayed her exasperation. "Go."

Karma and Ridge hiked in relative silence back into the main part of town and worked their way cautiously to the trailer park.

Her temper kept the bitter cold from registering. She tried not to pay attention to her trailer, which, by the looks of it, took the brunt of the damage within the compound.

"I really pissed them off this time, huh?" Karma laughed. "You know, as much as I don't want to go back in there, I'd like the chance to piss them off again."

Ridge laughed with her. "That's my girl." He pressed a kiss against her hair, then stepped away. "I'll check the right side of Jacob's trailer; you check the left."

Karma wound her way around the side of the trailer, checking high and low for any message, but came up empty.

The front door to Jacob's trailer stood open, hanging on a single hinge.

She signaled to Ridge to wait outside and made her way to the door. She'd picked up Malcolm's scent around the perimeter of the dented and rusty trailer, but inside, the air was permeated with it. "Come out, Malcolm. I'm here. What is your plan?"

Malcolm peeked his head around the door frame, his eyes squinting in the dim light of the morning. His eyes rose above her, meeting Ridge's. "They came last night. I'd gotten most of the people moved out of Finley by that time. Without your warning, we'd have been captured. Thank you." By his expression, the words tasted bitter in his mouth. He didn't want to have to thank Ridge for anything.

Ridge stepped up beside her and nodded.

Surveying the area, Malcolm stepped from the trailer, cautiously approaching them. "Did you see any of them on your way here?"

"No."

"Are you sure?"

Ridge shifted his body, turning so his back was to her, trusting her to watch Malcolm.

"This isn't my first rodeo, Malcolm. I'm not stupid enough to let the goon squad follow me. I've stayed out of their grasp for more than five years. I'd think if I were sloppy enough to let them follow me, they'd have caught me long before now." Karma adjusted her stance. "You should call out your minions. I can smell them. I don't like being surrounded."

Malcolm waved his hand around in some signal, and the others, including Jacob, appeared from under, around, and inside surrounding trailer shells.

She turned her back on Malcolm and walked across the trailer park grounds to a clearing. Karma plopped onto the ground and stretched her legs out in front of her, leaning back on her hands. "Sit down. All of you. We'll discuss the plan."

"Look, I'm the one who gathered all this information. I'm in charge here." Malcolm's voice held the pouting of a petulant child.

Karma raised her eyebrow and stared him down. "You may have gathered the information, assuming it is still where you left it. But *you* left it behind, and

I'm the one who knows how to get in and out of the building. If you think you can do it better, then you don't need me, and we are done here."

"Wait!" Malcolm huffed, and the others grumbled. "Fine! What's your plan then?"

"I need more information first. Where are the files you stashed?"

"I told you; they are on the seventh floor."

"Is the seventh floor a single room with a neon sign pointing to where you hid them? If not, I need more details."

"What's to stop you from going in there and taking the files for yourself, leaving us behind with nothing to show for it?"

"If you aren't going to give me some trust, this won't work. *You* came to *me*. Not the other way around."

"Guarantee me that you get the files for me, hand them over, and get us back out."

Karma laughed. "Are you kidding me? I can't guarantee I'll be able to get *myself* out of there. What makes you think I can make promises? And if you don't trust me to have details, why would you trust my word when it comes to your safety?" She turned to look at Ridge. "Is he serious?"

She stood up and brushed the dirt off her pants. "I have more reason than any of you to make sure I leave that facility alive. I won't stop fighting until I am free or I am dead. You can believe it or not. The longer we argue about this, the less time we have to prepare. I want to be far the hell away from here by first light tomorrow. Make your decision and make it soon. I don't have to go back into that place. I'm just as happy to leave without ever setting eyes on that cursed building again."

Ridge, having gotten to his feet when she did, stepped in front of her, a barrier between her and Meg, who'd stood at the same moment.

Meg made her way to Malcolm and crouched down, whispering something in his ear.

White lanced across his cheeks as Malcolm clenched his teeth together.

Jacob's steps were timid as he approached. He pointed at Karma and bent, whispering in Malcolm's other ear. He waved his hand, indicating Ridge, and continued.

"Fine!" Malcolm threw his hands into the air, exasperation oozing off him. "What do you need from me?"

"I need a layout of the seventh floor. A general location of where the documents are. If I know these things, they can help me find the best way in."

"You've moved around in the ceiling a lot. Can't you get into any room that way?" Ridge asked.

"At least the way the second floor is set up, the walls in the most secure rooms go all the way up to the next floor. The only way into those high-security rooms is through the door," she answered.

"What are they doing in those rooms?"

Malcolm shrugged. "I think at least some of the rooms are labs, where they are creating the serums to use on the people who are signing up to be guinea pigs."

"Signing up? I came in asking for help with food and supplies. I didn't 'sign up' to be experimented on, tortured!"

"We're told that you have all voluntarily signed up for this," Malcolm said defensively.

"Up on the seventh floor, the screams of agony are probably muffled enough that you don't hear them."

"This isn't getting us anywhere," Jacob interjected.

"There are records rooms on the seventh. I think they are built the same way as the labs. There are strict protocols on the doors for access, and a lot of the rooms are monitored by guards and/or cameras. Most of the records rooms and labs are right on top of one another from floor to floor." Malcolm drew the outline of the building in the dirt with his finger. The rooms he outlined in the middle of the building were the ones with the highest security. The ones she'd not been able to access on the second floor during her attempts years ago.

"Brute force will set off alarms, and contrary to your belief, I think your access card will either be useless or set off its own alarms. How do you anticipate getting around that?" Karma asked.

A grin crossed Malcolm's face, and he pointed to Allie.

Chapter 24

7619

Ridge

The chill bit into Ridge's skin, but he kept moving in the deepening shadows. The thick cloud cover, promising rain, further dampened the light from the sun. With the chillier temperatures came longer nights, and that would help them stay hidden as the group approached the train yard on the opposite side of the Phoenix Corps compound from Finley Avenue. At this rate, they'd be inside the building shortly before full darkness fell.

Their ragtag group made little sound as they weaved through, over, and around the wreckage of passenger and freight trains littering the area.

The passenger trains were once opulent, featuring lush fabrics in rich hues of red and blue. Fine metal fixtures were oxidized into dull colors and rough textures. The smell inside some of the cars made him gag. Years of dampness turned the padding and fabrics to mold, mildew, and rot. Evidence that animals had found their way into the overturned and damaged train cars littered the area, adding their own funk to the putrid mixture.

Crates were smashed to bits, and anything usable taken. Shards of wood and metal stuck to the soles of his boots, not strong enough or long enough to penetrate the thick soles. Forced to pause, they plucked the pieces of debris from their boots before continuing through the trainyard.

Karma led the way, her head on a swivel as she scanned for cameras or other devices that could signal they knew she had used this as a means of entry. She kept moving, so he assumed she hadn't seen anything alarming.

Ridge brought up the rear, keeping an eye on the companions neither of them trusted.

They shuffled their way up to the fence line at the edge of the Phoenix Corps compound.

Hearing Karma swear, Ridge weaved his way up to the fence alongside her.

"They repaired this section of fence."

"They repaired a lot of the holes in the fences over the last few months. I think it was a general precaution because they didn't know how you were getting in, so they tried to find all the weaknesses," Malcolm responded.

Karma looked around. "I'll go up and over. I can head to the entrance I'd planned to use and make sure they haven't closed it or set up cameras along the way."

"No."

Karma placed her hand on Ridge's forearm, stalling any further argument. "I'll be careful. I know this way well. If they've changed or added anything else, I'll get out of there immediately."

Ridge pulled her against him roughly, planting a hard kiss on her lips. "Come back here, or I'm coming in after you."

"I won't go in without you."

He knew she could've scaled the fence without his help, but it gave him something to do.

She removed the outer layer of flannel she wore, laying it over the barbed wire coiled along the top of the fence, and carefully picked her way over. Her head moved on a swivel, never staying in one spot long, surveying everything within sight.

A dull thud sounded when her feet hit the grass-covered ground at the base of the fence. "No additional cameras that I can see. Stay here. I'll be back in a few." She lowered into an army crawl and worked her way, low in the grass, until she disappeared over a slight rise in the terrain.

Ridge paced along the fence line. Anxiety rolled through his body. At one point, he curled his fingers through the chain link fencing, desperate to climb over.

"She said to wait," Malcolm said impatiently, grabbing the edge of Ridge's flannel.

The snarl on his face when he spun to face Malcolm had the man backing away and his minions stepping up.

"Keep your hands to yourself, or risk losing them," Ridge growled, rolling his shoulders to ease some of the tension building there.

Not two minutes later, he was back to pacing and searching the rise for any sign of Karma returning.

The shadows around him grew longer as interminable minutes ticked by. Having waited as long as he could, Ridge spun around, intent on scaling the fence when Karma reappeared, walking along the fence line toward him, minus yet another layer of flannel.

He closed the distance between them, scooping her up into his arms and burying his nose at the base of her neck, inhaling her scent and finally calming his nerves. When he was confident he could speak without shouting, he said, "What the hell took so long?"

Karma stayed in the circle of his arms, which he was grateful for. He didn't think he would be able to release her. Fear had ridden him hard in her absence. "The way is still open. I don't see any additional signs of cameras or other security measures. But, since they repaired the fence and we have to climb it anyway, I found a better place for us to go over." Her eyes shifted to where her shirt still hung on the barbed wire.

"I'll grab it. You rest for a minute." With his height, Ridge only needed to scale about halfway up the fence to grab and untangle Karma's shirt. He wrapped it back around her the moment his feet were back on solid ground. His hands ran up and down her arms to try to help warm her up.

"There aren't cameras. Once we get over the fence, we'll need to stay low. The entrance is fairly narrow.

The biggest of you will have a tight squeeze, but I'm confident we will all fit."

"How far is it? You're sure there aren't cameras? What if you missed some?" Malcolm quizzed her.

"If they saw me on a camera I didn't notice, then we might have a group of people waiting for us when we cross over. We're going to have to fight our way out. That's inevitable. Hopefully, we don't have to fight our way in."

"I thought you could get us in and out safely?" Malcolm's voice rose.

Ridge had to stifle his need to punch the scrawny, terrified pencil-pusher.

"I said I could possibly get you in and out. Safety wasn't ever going to be an option. It never is when Phoenix Corps is involved."

Malcolm glanced at Ridge and stiffened, probably reading the threat clearly written there, and backed up.

"Enough arguing! We are wasting time," Jacob said, stepping forward. "I don't want to be here any longer than I have to!"

Karma turned. "Follow or don't, Malcolm. I'm here; I'm going in." She started up the fence line.

The others lined up behind her, and Ridge brought up the rear.

They'd walked a fair distance before her dark blue flannel came into view on top of the barbed wire above the chain link fencing.

Ridge could see the hint of a small shed-like structure just beyond a rise in the ground.

Karma scaled the fence easily but stayed at the top. She waved to the others, indicating they should start their climb. One by one, Karma helped them over the barbed wire and down the other side.

They stood with their backs against the fencing while they waited for the rest to cross.

Once Ridge was over the barbed wire, he collected Karma's other flannel and handed it down to her. He landed on his feet beside her a moment later as Karma added the layer to the others she wore. "What's next?" he asked in a whisper.

"We head to the building there," she pointed in the direction of the roofline he'd seen. "Everyone, stay as low to the ground as you can. There's no cover on this side of the building. Keep your movements small."

Karma led the way again. Ridge directed the others to spread out a bit to the sides, forming a rough diamond shape that undulated over the ground as they crawled.

As they crested the rise, a sturdy brick shed with a solid steel door came into view.

Ridged sped up, working his way to the front with Karma. "How do you plan to get through that steel door?" he whispered.

"Ye of little faith. Trust me."

"I do. But..." Ridge waved his hand toward the solid-looking building.

Karma just shook her head and kept moving. It wasn't until she was close enough to reach out and touch the wall of the shed that Karma stood. She kept her back to the wall and slid along, motioning the others to do the same. Peeking around the corners and finding nothing, Karma moved to the door and easily pulled it open. She held it, motioning for the others to quickly enter the small room, which was filled with pipes and gauges.

"They leave this unlocked?" Malcolm asked.

Karma shook her head. "Nope." Her finger tapped on a piece of steel gray duct tape across the catch on the door, the exact color of the door itself.

Ridge surveyed the room they occupied. Four solid walls and the door. Pipes along the other three walls. "How exactly do you use this shed to get inside? I know I can't fit inside any of these pipes. You said it might be a tight fit for some of us, but there's no way." He pointed at the largest of the pipes to emphasize his point.

Karma patted his raised bicep with her hand and smiled. "Not through a pipe." She crouched down where a collection of pipes came through the floor and tucked her fingers into a crack in the concrete.

The concrete had a spiderweb of cracks running through it, and the one Karma manipulated looked no different than the rest. The instant it started to move, Ridge was beside her, helping to take the load when the gap was big enough for his fingers to fit in.

The slab of concrete weighed a ton, but they managed to lift it and lean it against the wall. Beneath was some hard-packed dirt and a narrow, concrete-lined channel through which the pipes ran that dropped into the ether of darkness beyond. He couldn't see any light below to indicate depth.

Karma tapped him on the shoulder to get his attention. "I'm going in first. I'll make sure nothing has changed. Once everyone else has come down, I'll need your help to replace the slab. This is only an entrance for me. I've never been able to climb back up to get out. We may never need it again, but I want to make sure that it's still hidden when we leave. Just in case."

"How far down is it?" he asked.

"About a twenty-five-foot drop from here. Fifteen from the bottom of the pipes. I usually close it off before I drop from the pipes."

"Lead the way."

Chapter 25

5713

Karma

Karma slid down the thick pipe into the darkness below. Maintenance lights used to illuminate the way, but the tunnel was nearly pitch-black now. A faint glow down the way told her that the lights were working further up the tunnel, but none of the ones here were on. Either a breaker blew, leaving this section of lights out, or they were off on purpose, and she was about to walk into a trap. She planned for the latter but hoped for the former.

"Ready?" Ridge called down the chase.

"The lights are out. Let my eyes adjust. I'll let you know." She kept her voice low, not wanting it to carry down the tunnel. The scents in this area were old and stale. There was a slight hint of her own scent, from her trip through here months ago. The air in here didn't move much, so while she didn't think anyone else had been down here since, she couldn't be sure. Karma squinted her eyes and surveyed her surroundings. She paid particular attention to the juncture of the walls and ceiling, looking for anything out of the ordinary, or different in texture from the rest, even a tell-tale sheen that could indicate a camera lens.

The waiting gave her eyes a chance to adjust, and it gave Phoenix Corps plenty of time to come at her, if they were keeping tabs on the area. She'd rather they take her and give the others a chance to get away. Ridge wouldn't have liked it, which was why she didn't tell him.

"I think we are okay," Karma said, her face raised to the chute, so her voice would carry to Ridge's heightened sense of hearing. "When you get down here, take a second look. Your eyes are better in the dark than mine."

Karma stepped out from beneath the concrete chase to make room for whoever descended to drop to the ground. Jacob's "Oomph!" as he hit the ground echoed through the tunnel.

Karma held out a hand and helped him back to his feet and away from the bottom of the chute. "Wait here quietly, while the rest of them make their way down. Sound carries. I don't want to alert anyone in the maintenance rooms that we are in here, if we can help it."

One by one, the others joined them until finally Ridge's feet hit the ground with a thud. "I don't see anything to cause alarm."

"Ok, help me back into the chute so that I can close up the concrete."

Ridge lifted her onto his shoulders and steadied her while she worked her way into a standing position at his shoulders.

She was still too far to grab the bottom of the pipe. "I need to get higher."

Ridge lifted her foot onto one of his hands and waited until she followed suit with the other.

Karma wobbled a bit as he slowly raised his hands above his head, holding her like she was on a cheerleading team. A bounce from him was enough for her to wrap her fingers around one of the pipes. She pulled her feet from Ridge's hands and swung her legs up and around the pipe as well. Karma worked her way around until she was upright and shimmied her way up the pipe until she was high enough to reach the concrete slab above.

She locked her legs around the pipe and struggled to move the slab. Some of her strength was back, but not all of it, and her stamina was much lower than she was used to. The slab settled into place with a louder thud than she intended, but at least it was back in place. Karma relaxed her legs a bit and slid back down the pipe. Ridge caught her before she hit the floor, once she dropped off the pipe.

"You okay?" he asked.

Karma nodded but didn't stop moving. They were in here now, until they found a way out.

Ridge grabbed her hand before she took another step. "We'll get you out of here. I promise."

She couldn't speak; her anxiety threatened to choke her.

His lips descended on hers, and the world faded away. It was just him, just her—no Phoenix Corps. No Malcolm. No worries.

Karma took a deep, shaky breath when he pulled back.

"You've got this. In and out, like you've always done. We're just shopping for something new this time."

Karma squeezed his hand and nodded, then took her place at the head of the group. "This room dumps into a corrugated metal tube. You'll need to crouch. And be quiet. Everything echoes and carries the sound straight into the maintenance rooms." She purposely faced away from the tube when she spoke.

A split second later, before she lost her nerve, Karma re-entered the tube for what she hoped would be the final time.

While the others behind her walked carefully, the noise pounded in her head, drowning out the sound of her heartbeat. Rationally, she knew they weren't being that loud, but the minute noises had her grinding her teeth and fighting herself to not make even more noise by shouting at them to be quiet. The loudest noises came from the unaltered—Malcolm, Allie, and Jacob. None of them had the training to keep their steps light and cover their tracks.

Up ahead, in the next section, the blue glow of the maintenance lights made it much easier to navigate the corrugated tunnels.

They were about three sections of tube away from where she'd left the tunnel the last time she'd been here. Karma did *not* want to take that route again, so she veered off to the right, into a smaller tunnel, following a different set of pipes—water pipes instead of electrical conduits. Grabbing one of the brackets holding the pipes to the ceiling, Karma hauled herself up and into a narrow offshoot. There was grumbling behind her, she assumed from Duke, and she heard Ridge tell the guy "Shut it."

A few minutes later, she came upon what she was looking for. Her shoulders ached from army crawling the whole distance, as well as through the yard on the surface. Soreness on the inner sides of her elbows told her she'd probably blistered and worn the human skin away in that place, leaving her osteoderms exposed and the skin around the spot very tender. With her smaller stature, it was easier for her to navigate these tunnels. She could understand the frustrations of the others, but they couldn't afford to put voice to those frustrations right now.

Karma used the brackets again for leverage and quietly lowered herself into the maintenance room she made it to.

The pipes split inside and went in all sorts of directions. Some went into giant well-like structures, pouring countless gallons inside.

The water being pumped into this room was intended for the citizens of Fairway. It was supposed to be distributed to the people here until Phoenix Corps could repair the infrastructure, and people could once again have running water in their homes.

Karma frowned at the pipes heading up into the ceiling and to other parts of the building. She turned to Allie. "How long do we have after you've set a charge before it blows? And, how big of a bang are we talking?"

Allie swung her gaze to Malcolm and waited for his nod of approval before she answered. "About thirty minutes is the longest I can set it for. And, as for how big a bang, how big do you need it?"

"A small one. For thirty minutes." Karma looked at Malcolm. "This is the main water supply into the building. Taking it out will do two things: it will bring everyone running *here* while we are on the seventh floor, and disrupting their water supply will cripple part of the facility, at least for a while." Focusing again on Allie, "We need it big enough to damage the pipes and be heard a few floors away, but not so big that it collapses this part of the facility. I don't plan to come back through here, but it will be a game-time decision on how we get the hell out when we are done."

She nodded and pulled off her backpack, rooting around a rats' nest of wires. Jacob pulled off his pack and opened it, revealing what Karma assumed was the actual explosive materials.

"We need to hurry, Allie," Jacob said. "Where's the best place to put it?"

Allie pulled what she needed out of her bag and walked to the largest pipe in the room. "This one. We'll put a lovely little hole in this massive pipe. With the amount of water pushing through it, we'll have this floor flooded in no time, even with a small hole."

"I don't want it to be an easy fix," Karma chimed in.

"Oh, I'll make it difficult." An evil smile stole over Allie's face, and she rubbed her hands together like a master villain.

"Do it."

Allie knelt at a ninety-degree turn in the pipe, with a tee branching off nearby, and went to work.

Karma watched in fascination as Allie's nimble hands worked the explosive substance and the wires. Quicker than she thought possible, Allie was done, and they were ready to move.

"You have thirty minutes to get us out of here."

Karma nodded. She knew a way out of the room. It wasn't one she'd used more than a couple of times, so she hoped nothing had changed.

Karma climbed on top of one of the huge vats of water and poked her head up into the drop ceiling. As usual, wires and pipes crisscrossed the space above. Setting her feet on the top of the closest wall, she held onto one of the steel supports and reached for the next person.

"Don't put any weight on the ceiling. It won't hold you. Keep your weight on the tops of the walls, or on the support beams." One by one, Karma helped the others into the gap in the ceiling. She kept her eyes peeled for any indication that there was new surveillance within the ceiling.

They climbed over and through the obstacles in the ceiling until they reached the far corner. They'd needed to stop several times, hearing voices from the floor below them, and waited for the voices to fade away before moving again.

At the corner, rebar in a U-shape was embedded into the concrete wall, forming a crude ladder within another concrete-lined chase. The climb over had taken much longer than she wanted. They needed to hurry if they were going to get to the seventh floor before the explosion went off.

Chapter 26

Ridge

The hair on the back of his neck rose as he climbed the rebar ladder. There were too many of them. If they got caught, their increased number *might* come in handy, but that increased number was likely to get them caught.

Ridge fought the urge to grumble at Malcolm's minions in front of him to hurry up. They had a long way to climb and not much time.

On each floor, he scanned the area surrounding the ladder to ensure there were no cameras pointed at them.

He'd just reached the opening where they could move into the ceiling of the fourth floor above ground when the pipes blew. Ridge struggled to block out the sound of the alarms blaring around them. The piercing sound grated on his nerves and hurt his ears.

Shouts were indistinguishable beneath the blaring alarms.

Ridge pushed at the foot of Meg, urging her to keep climbing. She glared down at him, but he didn't back down. "Move!" he mouthed at her and pointed up.

Karma was probably already two to three floors above him. The idea of her moving out into danger without him right behind gripped his heart like a vise. He needed to be back here, to watch her back with these unknown allies, but everything within him screamed to get to her side.

Although the alarm was still enough to hurt his ears, when he made it to the fifth floor, it dulled enough for him to hear the stomping of boots in the hallway below.

Did they know what was happening? Had he missed cameras? Had Karma heard them?

Ridge drove his way past the woman in front of him, pushing her off to the side as he climbed past her. He propelled himself up the ladder.

He breathed a sigh of relief when his hand closed around Karma's ankle.

She looked down at him, startled.

"There aren't usually goon squad members up on these floors. At least not while I was still here. I heard their boots on the fifth floor. Either they are expecting us,"—he paused, glancing down the ladder at the others, then meeting her eyes again—"or they've upped their security since we were last in here."

Karma squinted and scanned the area they could see. "Either way, we're here. We're not leaving until we get what we came for."

"I don't trust Malcolm."

"I don't trust him either. But we're here and we'll take down anyone who stands in the way." Karma moved up another rung and stepped out onto the top of a nearby wall. "Make sure the others get off the ladder without going through the ceiling." She dropped a quick kiss on his lips and headed out into the maze of steel supports, wires, and pipes.

Ridge hung onto the ladder with one hand and one foot, scooching to the side to give room for the others to bypass him. He directed them where to put their feet so that they could follow Karma deeper into the floor.

One by one, they exited the ladder area and made their way to a concrete block wall that Karma stopped next to. The wall went clear to the next floor and above. They were all balanced precariously on the narrow top of a wall that ran parallel to it. The space between the two walls must have been the hallway.

Karma started to lift the corner of one of the ceiling tiles to peer into the hallway, but Ridge shook his head, and she paused.

"At least two directly below us," he mouthed and motioned with his hands.

She settled the tile back down and picked her way farther down a perpendicular wall. Karma lifted another tile, just enough to see there wasn't any light coming from below. An instant later, she lifted the tile fully and dropped through.

No sounds of scuffling reached him, but it didn't stop the lump in his throat from threatening to choke him.

One at a time, each of the others dropped in behind her, leaving Ridge the last in the ceiling.

He didn't drop down.

Ridge shuffled back to where the two walls met and listened carefully for any sound of boots. Muffled thuds indicated they were around a corner and at the far end of that hall. He made his way back, dropped down, and relayed the information to Karma and replaced the ceiling tile they'd dropped through.

She nodded. Karma proceeded to the door and stopped with her hand on the handle. Motioning for Ridge to come closer, to listen at the door again, she held her other hand up to keep the others in place and quiet.

At his signal, Karma dragged the door open as quietly as she could.

The patrol they'd been waiting for had just passed the heavy metal door.

Ridge grabbed the first guy by the throat and yanked him into the room.

Before the second guard had a chance to react, Karma jumped onto his back, pulling him backward until her feet hit the ground, and he was nearly bent in half. With her arm closing off his airway, he couldn't scream. Using his awkward positioning and her increased strength, Karma wrestled him into the room.

Ridge wasn't prepared for the giant fist that narrowly missed his face, slamming into the temple of the large guard he held. The guard went limp in his hands and slid to the ground.

Duke nodded.

"Thanks."

He turned to help Karma, but Meg already had the guard knocked out and tied up with his own zip ties.

"That is why we brought them," Malcolm whispered, pointing at the two, now slumped, guards in the corner of the room.

"When they wake up, they'll be a problem," Duke grumbled.

"That was you less than a year ago," Meg pointed out. "I could've killed you. I did kill your partner."

Duke rolled his eyes.

"We don't have time for this." He pushed his way past them and back to the door to listen.

Lighter footsteps were making their way down the hall, and a slight clicking sound accompanied them.

Malcolm stepped up beside him. "It's another pencil pusher. She worked with me. Had an annoying habit of clicking her pen *all damn day.* Not Altered. Not a threat."

"Did she have access to the room you hid your files in?" Karma asked quickly.

Malcolm shook his head.

Karma's hand rested on Ridge's forearm for a moment. "Let her go past. Don't grab her. Just tell us when she's gone."

When the sounds faded around the next corner, Ridge gave the all-clear.

Chapter 27

5713

Karma

Pushing out in front of Ridge the second he gave the all clear, Karma kept her head turned down and away from the cameras she knew hovered in each of the corners. She hoped people were still too preoccupied with their earlier explosion, but she wasn't going to bet on it.

She pulled Malcolm out with her and dragged him over to the door of the room he indicated. "Here?"

At his nod, Allie stepped forward, with Jacob on her heels.

"Wait a second," Karma said, holding up her hand. "Another explosion will bring people running here. Let me see if I can break the lock first."

"We don't have time for this!" Malcolm shouted.

Ridge pinned him to the wall in the hallway with his hand covering Malcolm's mouth. "Shouting is as bad as blowing shit up. You want to bring the entire facility to this floor? We want to use stealth until it's no longer an option. Cooperate, or we'll leave you to do it yourself, and you can find your own way out."

Malcolm reached toward her but pulled his hand back when Ridge growled. "Let Jacob have a crack at it first."

Jacob stopped in front of the ID card reader and fished in Allie's pack. He pulled out a screwdriver and popped the front plate off, exposing a keypad. Hitting three buttons at once, a light appeared, blinking rapidly. He reinserted the screwdriver near the edge and popped the keypad off. Using wire strippers and alligator clips, Jacob stripped and joined two wires together.

An audible click, loud even to Karma's ears, echoed off the walls.

Jacob nodded at Malcolm, who pushed open the door and stepped into the darkened room.

He removed the clips, replaced the plates, and followed them inside. The magnetic lock reengaged the second the door latched.

Small windows looking out into the hallway let in a minute amount of light. Open shelves lined the walls, packed full of boxes, while rack after rack of servers hummed in multiple rows in the middle of the room. Blinking lights highlighted a rat's nest of wires going this way and that. A thin carpet covered the floors, muffling the sounds of their footsteps.

"Where is it, Malcolm?" Karma asked.

Malcolm pointed to a large cabinet in the far corner. He approached the deep gray cabinet like a ticking time bomb. He jiggled the handle, but it didn't move.

"I thought you said you hid it. Anyone could have taken it out of there if you just left it in a cabinet."

Karma read the panic in Malcolm's eyes as he wiggled the handle again and again.

"Get what you need so that we can get out of here."

Malcolm reached out, grabbing the sleeve of Meg's shirt, dragging her closer. "You're up."

Meg rubbed her hands together and cracked her knuckles. She pulled two thin picks out of her back pocket and crouched until she was eye level with the lock. Inserting the pins, she tilted her head and listened as she maneuvered and jiggled the pins until she was satisfied. She pushed down on the handle, and the door popped open a second later.

Malcolm eased open the cabinet door and pulled out one of the center shelves, handing it off to Jacob, then knocked a few times on the side panel, where it rested against the wall. The third knock echoed back, followed by a creaking noise as he pried open a hidden compartment and pulled out a manila envelope stuffed full to bursting.

Jacob took the folder and slid it into his pack.

Karma breathed a sigh of relief and moved to leave the room. Malcolm gripped her upper arm with bruising strength, much harder than she'd thought him capable.

"Remove your hand or lose it." Fury infused Ridge's voice.

Karma twisted her arm out of Malcolm's hold. "We got what we came for. We need to get out as quickly as possible."

Thundering footsteps echoed in the hall.

"We didn't make noise," Jacob's voice trembled.

"Probably cameras." Karma shifted her body to face the door. "We're pinned in here. There's no other door. It will funnel them through the lone door, but we have no way to get out except through them."

The security panel outside the door beeped repeatedly as they tried to gain entry to the room.

"I didn't reconnect the wires. The keypad is useless."

Loud bangs vibrated the whole area as goon squad members pummeled the door from their side, rattling the hinges and hitting hard enough to dent the door.

"Duke, Meg, fan out beside us," Ridge ordered.

"We don't take orders from you." Duke sounded like a petulant child.

"Help us fight or get the hell out of the way." Karma's patience for these guys was at an end.

The steel door groaned as the goon squad on the other side of the door pried it open. Through the window, more goon squad members filled the hallway.

The gap in the doorway was shoved open enough for the first man to push his way into the room.

Ridge stepped forward, blocking the fist flying at him.

The second guy through the door carried a taser and lunged.

A screeching sound ripped through the room as Meg tore a hunk of steel from one of the server rack's supports and swung the rod, knocking the taser to the ground, sending it spinning away. The man cradled his mangled hand against his body and kicked at Duke.

A woman climbed through the door next with her eyes locked on Karma.

Annabeth.

Fangs extended and venom dripping, Annabeth lunged over the others who were grappling between them.

Karma relaxed her knees and let Annabeth's shoulder catch her across the chest. Using Annabeth's momentum against her, Karma rolled her back to the floor and added more force with her legs, propelling Annabeth past her and into the first rack of servers. The impact sent the first row, already weakened from the piece Meg ripped off, toppling into the next and into the next like dominoes.

Deafening crashes rolled over the room and out into the hallway, vibrating the entire floor.

Blood seeped from a cut above Ridge's eye and the corner of his mouth from a split lip. His fight shifted closer to the doorway, and he threw his adversary into a cabinet, toppling it in front of the door, blocking more reinforcements from entering the room.

Duke's arm dripped blood from three deep gashes caused by claws from the feline Altered he battled. Meg fought next to him, a matching set of gashes in her thigh.

Taking advantage of Karma's inattention, Annabeth struck out, her fangs sinking deeply into Karma's ankle. The bite easily penetrated her human skin but bounced and scraped against her osteoderms until one sank between two plates. Karma ripped her leg away, fire slowly spreading up her calf.

Annabeth lunged at her again. A sharp fang sliced through several layers of her clothes but failed to do more than scrape the human skin beneath.

Karma grabbed Annabeth's blonde hair, wrapping it around her fist and hauling her head out of striking range. Reaching in with her other hand, she ripped out one fang, followed by the other.

Annabeth screamed in frustration and pain, frantically swinging her arms as she attempted to knock Karma away.

Karma elbowed Annabeth in the nose and tossed her back into the pile of servers, reaching for the taser the second attacker dropped, tucking it into the waistband of her pants.

She'd lost track of Jacob and Allie in the chaos, the fight claiming her attention, until a shouted, "Get down!" came out of the darkness.

Jacob's body slammed into her side, knocking her against the wall. Allie had done the same to Malcolm.

Ringing stifled her hearing. Dust and debris choked her lungs and clouded her vision.

Frantic pulling at her arm urged her to her feet.

They needed to move, but she wouldn't leave without Ridge. Karma pulled away, back in the last direction she'd seen Ridge. She barely recognized him under the fine dust sticking to his blood and sweat, covering his dark hair and obscuring his features.

He moved next to her, pulling Malcolm behind him, and she turned back to Jacob, following him and Allie over dust, debris, and ravaged servers through the enormous hole they'd blown in the far, concrete block wall of the room.

Fluorescent lights swung wildly in the hall. Through the dusty air, the outline of a debris pile blocking both sides of the hallway was visible. Parts of the ceiling grid hung drunkenly. Duke, who had stumbled out of the hole behind Ridge, catapulted himself into the air and grabbed another area of the grid, yanking more of it down in both directions, giving the pile of debris an additional obstacle to climb over.

The door opposite the hole dangled precariously from half a hinge. Inside, a woman gaped at them, her mouth opening and closing like a fish.

"Hey Betsy, long time no see, huh?" Malcolm saluted her and strode past the frozen woman.

Duke crowded into her personal space. He lowered his mouth to her ear and whispered, too low for Karma to make out the words. Producing some sort of ID from his pocket, he showed it to her and discreetly pointed at each of the group. His eyes shifted from hers to the group and the hallway a couple of times, then he motioned for her to go out the door, away from the office they occupied.

Once she was out of earshot, Duke showed the others.

A flawless fake.

"What did you tell her?"

"I've caught you stealing and am holding you in this room until my backup can get through the dust and debris you used to slow us down. Also, she'll be greatly rewarded if she points my backup in this direction." His cocky wink made her want to smack him. He turned to Karma and pointed at the ceiling tile in the far corner of the room, still intact. "Up and out?"

Karma stumbled a step, and Ridge caught her, concern readable on his features, even obscured by the dust.

"I'll be fine. Keep moving." Karma couldn't tell if her vision was blurred due to the explosion aftermath or from her reaction to the venom, but either way, it really didn't matter; they needed to keep moving.

With half of the ceiling ripped down, there was nothing to keep the dirt and dust from the ceiling cavity, so they couldn't see any better up there as they breached the ceiling of the office and climbed up.

Dizziness caused her to grab onto pipes periodically, keeping her from tumbling off the narrow paths and through the ceiling. She pushed herself harder, faster to make it to one of the ladders. Nausea rolled through her.

Karma had just reached the ladder when commotion sounded behind them. Turning her head revealed the cause.

Dozens of goon squad members converged from every direction in the ceiling.

She pushed Malcolm and the others onto the ladder, encouraging them to descend as quickly as possible. Ridge stopped next to her, just as Allie reached for the first rung.

Allie reached out for Karma's hand and placed a small device into her hand. She pointed to the base of the floor above. "Place it before you start to descend. Move fast. You won't have long."

Ridge nudged her toward the ladder, his back to her, prepared to go to battle against the entire goon squad. "Go."

"You first." Karma grabbed him by the back of his shirt and pulled, catching him off guard. He dropped down four rungs before he caught himself.

She climbed one rung higher and pushed the explosive device into a small crevice. The goon squad was closing in fast, and she needed to move. Her hands were clammy, and another wave of dizziness and nausea threatened to stop her in her tracks. She'd only made it down three rungs when her hands slipped.

Chapter 28

Ridge

Ridge kept an eye on Karma. Something didn't feel right with her. She seemed unsteady on her feet. With the dust from the last explosion sticking to them, he couldn't judge her complexion to see if she was pale, and he hadn't been close enough to feel if she was burning up.

With the goon squad now navigating the ceiling and closing the distance between them, Ridge sped up, moving the others along faster. Malcolm didn't like taking orders. Duke and Meg weren't any better. And Ridge was running out of patience.

Sounds of the goon squad closing in made him raise his head, in time to see Karma slump and collapse, falling backward from the ladder. They'd barely made it to the ceiling of the sixth floor.

Ridge let go of the rung he held and fell away from it. He locked Karma's back to his chest and curled up to protect the back of his head as they fell away from the wall and through the sixth-floor ceiling to the concrete floor below, taking the impact on his back.

The air rushed out of his lungs, and high-pitched screams from the women, sitting at desks in the room they landed in, assaulted his already abused eardrums. He shifted to his side, keeping Karma in his arms, as debris from the ceiling fell all around and on them.

"Run!" Ridge shouted at the women.

They'd been frozen in place but scampered out of the room at his shout.

Ridge wiped his hand across Karma's face, smearing more dirt than he removed. She wasn't hot to the touch, but cold and clammy. Colder than she should have been.

The racket from the ceiling pulled his attention. Several men descended the ladder.

Ridge groaned as he got to his feet, the bruises and aches from his fall screaming in protest. He lifted

Karma, tossing her over his shoulder in a fireman's carry and sprinting out the door, slamming it shut behind him.

He'd barely taken a step when the whole floor shook.

Shredded ceiling tiles rained down with more gray dust, choking them again. Screams came from every direction as people charged out of rooms and down halls. Rumbles above indicated huge chunks of rubble falling down the concrete shaft surrounding the ladder rungs. He hoped the others were able to get away before it blew.

Ridge kept his head down and tried to blend in with the other dust-covered and panicked people heading for the stairwells. Alarms blared on every floor, and he couldn't filter them out to hear other sounds. He'd learned to rely a lot on his ears over the years, and he had to push away the panic that they couldn't help him now. One step at a time. One problem at a time. He'd promised to get her out of this place if it was the last thing he did. Ridge wouldn't break that promise.

Halfway down the stairs to the fifth floor, Ridge moved to the corner of the landing, hiding his face as if he was coughing, while a team of Altereds shoved past the terrified employees fleeing the floor above. They never glanced in his direction.

Once the door to the floor above slammed shut, Ridge moved back into the flow of people descending. As his foot came down on another step, he heard Karma groan.

He raced down the other flights, pushing out onto the second floor, unwilling to go any further until he checked on her.

Her breathing was shallow, and her skin was clammy when he touched her. She groaned again and made a half-hearted attempt to cough.

Ridge sat her up and rubbed her back, trying to get her to breathe easier, cradling her in his lap. "Cough, baby," he encouraged. "Get that crap out of your lungs. Stay with me, please. I need your help to get out of here."

She turned her head into him, resting her cheek on his chest, and gave a weak cough.

He ran his knuckles down the center of her chest, hard.

Karma moaned and pushed into him, backing away from the pain stimulus.

"That's it, baby. Wake up and yell at me for that." He did it again.

Her eyes fluttered open, unseeing.

"Karma, can you tell me what's wrong?"

Her eyes closed again.

This time, when he repeated the motion with his knuckles, she slapped his hand away.

A harsh cough wracked her body. She opened her eyes and scanned the room. "Where are we?"

"Second floor."

"The others?"

"Not sure. You fell through the ceiling on the sixth floor. They were below us. Hopefully, they kept moving away and got to safety before the explosion blew."

She sat forward and climbed to her knees, her movements slow and jerky.

"What's wrong? "

She reached down, lifting the hem of her jeans. Blood oozed from a puncture wound on her leg; the area of human skin around it was fire red and streaked with white. "Annabeth. It's her venom." Karma must have read the panic in his face and placed her hand on his cheek. "It's not the first time I've been bitten by a snake with venom. It's not pleasant, but I'll survive."

He helped her to her feet.

"We can't stay here. We need to keep moving. I'll be okay."

Taking a few precious seconds, Ridge pulled her to him, wrapping his arms around her. "Where's the closest exit?"

"We need to find the others first."

"We *need* to get you out of here."

She stumbled when she stepped onto her injured leg but pushed him away when he tried to help her. Karma scrambled up onto a steel gray desk in the corner of the room and popped up the ceiling tile above. The cloud of debris dropped into the room, a gritty film covering the desk and floor below.

"I walked right past a squad of Altered on the stairs. They weren't paying attention. They couldn't tell the difference with everyone coated in this crap. Let's just go that way."

"The others were in the ceiling. That's our best bet for finding them. Once we get to them, maybe. But until then, I'm going up."

Knowing he'd never get her to listen, he put his effort into helping and lifted her into the cavity above. She still grabbed onto the structures around her for support more often than he liked, but she seemed steadier on her feet as they moved through.

When they reached the ladder, a massive chunk of concrete blocked the shaft.

Karma started down the ladder to the next floor. She paused as he made his way onto the rungs. "I told Malcolm we'd have the most options for escape from the first floor. We'll go down one and see if we can find evidence of them there."

He nodded and followed her lead. She knew the best ways; he'd follow her lead, even though every instinct screamed at him to get her out now.

Chapter 29

Karma

Karma stepped off the ladder and onto the wall of a storage room on the first floor. Her vision was still off, making her dizziness come and go in waves. The nausea was subsiding, but her leg was on fire.

A tile to the right had less debris on it than the others. She pointed out the discrepancy to Ridge.

He motioned for her to wait there while he went to check it out.

As much as she wanted to defy the instruction, she wasn't stupid. Her body was doing its best to fight off the venom's effects, but it left her at a disadvantage, vulnerable. And Ridge would step in if she got herself into a bad situation, risking himself. It would be smarter to let him look first.

Voices in raised whispers drifted through the ceiling tiles in the room below.

"No. She wouldn't leave us. We need to try to find them."

"If she's lucky, she's dead," came Malcolm's reply. "Give me the records. You can stay here and wait for her. We're leaving."

"No."

Sounds of a scuffle reached them.

Karma moved around Ridge and dropped from the ceiling onto the top of a shelf in the storage room holding the others. He landed behind her a split second later, and they both dropped to the floor.

Karma ripped the bag away from Malcolm and placed herself between the squabbling men. "Glad to see you, too."

Ridge placed himself at her back, his presence there keeping her upright as a wave of dizziness and blurred vision swept over her. Heat from his hand seeped through the layers of clothes she wore, steadying her. She blinked away the dizziness and refocused on the man in front of her, and the two of his allies who were stepping up to flank her and Ridge.

His hand curled into a fist at her back, and she dropped her chin a fraction of an inch to tell him she'd noticed, shifting her weight to the balls of her feet.

"I think this company wants to get its hands on you, Karma. If I hand you over to them, I'd be willing to bet they'd let the rest of us go waltzing out the front door."

Jacob and Allie looked confused, their heads swinging back and forth between Karma and Malcolm.

"I'd be willing to bet you won't survive that decision." Ridge's unyielding tone came out as more of a growl.

"Even if they'd be more lenient in exchange for me—which I highly doubt—do you really think they'd let you walk out knowing you stole from them?"

"What they don't know won't hurt them. I plan to make a huge profit from those documents. I'll be set for life."

A jerky head motion was the only warning before Duke and Meg lunged. Jacob's eyes widened, and he stepped back, pulling Allie with him.

Karma snap kicked Malcolm in the gut and ducked out of the way of Duke's meaty fist.

Ridge blocked a kick aimed at her from Meg and spun, slamming his forearm into Duke's throat.

Duke's back slammed into the door, the echo rolling down the hallway outside. They didn't have much time.

Karma's head spun through her mental map of this floor while dodging Malcolm. He was fast, but not strong.

Meg slipped away from fighting with Ridge and bee-lined for Jacob and Allie.

Karma fought off the dizziness and exhaustion pulling at her. She shifted her body, putting herself between Jacob and Meg.

Swiping a broom as she passed a rack of cleaning supplies, Meg swung the handle in an arc.

Karma took the hit on her shoulder, unable to dodge both the knife Malcolm pulled from thin air, and the attack from Meg. Nerves down her arm went dead from the impact. Her right arm hung uselessly at her side.

Meg spun with her momentum, readying for a second hit.

This time, Karma caught the handle with her left hand. The concussion of the hit sent pinpricks of pain from her hand up to her elbow. She ignored the pain and locked the handle under her arm, pinning it against her body.

When Meg yanked the handle back, Karma let go.

Meg's arms windmilled, falling backwards into another rack of supplies.

Karma advanced on her.

Using the handle like a fencing sword, Meg thrust it at her chest.

Shoving the handle down and away, Karma brought up her knee, snapping the handle, and spun, jabbing out with it.

The splintered end of the handle ripped through Malcolm's shirt, getting lodged just under his collarbone at his shoulder.

Malcolm tripped, slamming his injured shoulder into Duke, who'd been trying to back away from Ridge's vicious blows, and screamed in agony.

A cry of frustration blasted around the room, and Karma turned to the origin of the sound.

She choked, and her eyes burned relentlessly, blinded by a powdery white substance thrown by the screaming Meg. Meg stepped on some broken glass that had shattered when it was knocked off a nearby shelf during the scuffle. Judging by the sound, Karma shifted her weight to her back foot and leaned her body back. Air whooshed by her cheek when Meg's hit missed.

Karma threw her weight forward, catching Meg's abdomen with her shoulder. The audible blast of air rushed over the back of Karma's neck, and they tumbled to the ground. Grappling for position, Karma fought hard to keep the advantage of being on top. She slammed her elbow into Meg's face, hearing a satisfying crack and feeling sticky wetness against her skin. With her hand on Meg's throat, she felt the skin pull when Meg turned her head. Throwing another elbow, Karma connected with Meg's temple.

The fight left Meg's body.

Karma blindly crawled off Meg, hoping to avoid further injury as she made her way to where the slop sink would be.

Water barely trickled from the tap, and Karma groaned in frustration. Sounds of fists meeting flesh and grunts of pain ratcheted up her anxiety. She couldn't help Ridge if she couldn't see, and danger surrounded them.

Karma spun when a hand landed on her shoulder.

"Just me," Jacob quickly said and took her hand, turning it up, placing a heavy plastic jug there. "It's water."

Gratefully, Karma dumped the water over her face, sluicing it over her eyes to clear them of whatever awful chemical Meg used to douse her in. Grit still filled her eyes when she finished, and her vision was blurry, but she could see.

Malcolm's face was pale where he cowered next to the wall, his hand on the end of the broom handle protruding from his shoulder. Meg lay not far from her, out cold, and blood covered her face.

Thundering footsteps and shouts filtered through the door; time was up.

Ridge toppled a heavy shelf, knocking Duke to the ground and blocking the door, wedging it shut. He turned when she called out his name, then grabbed the taser she tossed out of the air, jamming into the side of Duke's neck.

The big man convulsed with the voltage entering his body, then lay still.

Making his way over the debris, Malcolm—who flinched away—and Meg's still form, Ridge checked her over for injuries.

"We need to get out of here. Now." Karma pointed at the door. "That's going to be a problem."

"Not really." Allie's small voice caught her attention.

Jacob held up two handfuls of what Allie had given her on the ladder to slow the others from following. Allie held up two more. "While you guys dealt with the Wonder Twins and their fearful idiot leader, we made ourselves useful."

"What's your plan?" Ridge asked.

Allie stepped up. "If we blow the door, we should at least delay those on the other side. On this floor, you said that there are a lot of places to get out, right?"

"We're on the ground floor here. Windows, doors, through the wall with your fancy explosives. It's all an option here," Karma answered.

"If we go a long way, winding around to pass as many structural walls as we can, and place these, we can bring the whole facility down around their ears."

Karma dropped her gaze to Malcolm, Duke, and the still unconscious Meg.

"Leave them." Ridge's hard stare cowed Malcolm even more.

"How many of the explosive charges do you have, and how many do we need?" Karma asked, her question punctuated with the screeching of metal against the tile floor.

The goon squad was pushing through the blockade.

"The more we have, the better, but we could spare a couple, I guess." Allie looked confused.

Karma held out her hand.

Allie placed two of them in her palm.

Kneeling in front of Malcolm, Karma held up one of the charges. "I'm placing this on the other side of the room. You follow us, I'll kill you. You find your own way out. I see hide or hair of you after this moment, and you'll never get the chance to regret it. Wake up the others or not, I don't care. Our working together has ended."

"My documents…"

"…Aren't yours any longer." Karma faced Jacob and Allie. "Where will be safest for us?"

Allie pointed at a corner flanked on either side by heavy-duty metal cabinets. "Here. Place the one near the door close to the hinge side of the jam. Place the other directly across from it." Allie held up a strange-looking box. I can set them off together with this. We'll need to start moving before the dust settles."

Ridge took one of the explosives out of her hand, hurried over and around the remains of the room to place it near the door.

Karma placed the other and met him, with Allie and Jacob on the other side of the room. She pulled him close. "Cover your ears."

Crouched down, she buried her face in his chest, bracing herself for the boom that followed.

She didn't look to see if Malcolm and the others were moving; she didn't care. Karma stepped over the carnage that remained of the room and hallway, squinting her already abused eyes to protect them from the dirt, debris, and dust in the air.

The fine dust on the floor tiles made them slippery in spots, and huge chunks of building materials created other obstacles. But they moved as efficiently as possible away from the pile of moaning bodies they'd left behind them. The further they moved from the storage room, the clearer the air became.

People who worked on this floor were mostly grunts and dock workers. This fight was above their pay grade, and they fled, not paying attention to the motley-looking crew running down the halls at them.

It took everything in her not to run for the first exit, to escape while they had the chance. Every instinct in her body wanted her to leave, but she pressed on, pushing the explosives into areas she thought would do the most damage.

The ghostly grey woman who stepped out of the stairwell as they rounded the next corner stopped her in her tracks.

Covered head to toe in the remains of the explosion from the server room on the seventh floor, Annabeth's reptilian eyes and fangs were the only recognizable aspects of her. The disturbing forked tongue Karma hadn't noticed until then poked out of her mouth. "I can taste your fear from here, Karma."

"Creepy *and* gross, Annabeth." Without turning around, Karma handed her remaining explosives to Jacob. Ridge made a move to step in front of her, but Karma stopped him with her arm. "Finish what we started. I'll meet you when I'm done here. Please." Karma pushed Jacob and Ridge to get them moving on the far side of the hallway, as far from Annabeth as she could keep them. Her hand on Allie's forearm, she stopped her for a second. "Five minutes. No more. Get out and set them off in five minutes."

"But..."

Karma shook her head, stopping his continued protests. She waited until Ridge started moving with Jacob, placing the next explosive. Karma lowered her voice so she hoped only Allie could hear. "Taking out this facility is more important than me. I'll get myself out. Five minutes. Don't let *anyone* stop you."

Allie nodded and hurried to catch up with the men.

Chapter 30

Karma

"You've always been so cocky," Annabeth sneered, disdain dripping from her voice.

"Phoenix Corps left me no choice. You only think about *yourself*. If you cared about anyone, even a hundredth of what you care about yourself, you would have been unstoppable. You could have helped so many—"

"Helped people? You took them away from their treatments, making them go mad! Watched us all suffer with barely enough food, no real resources. Phoenix Corps provides food, clean water, power, a real bed, and heat when it's cold."

"At what price? How many people don't survive the so-called 'treatments,' huh? I wasn't *asked* if I wanted to be part of their inhumane experiments. I didn't want to become one of their goons." Tick, tick, tick. Karma counted the seconds in her head. She didn't want to be in this building when they set off the explosion.

Annabeth smirked. "It's a price I'm glad I paid." She dove at Karma, her mouth open in a hiss. The stubs of her fangs dripped in her mouth, but without the points Karma had broken off earlier, they'd be useless.

Karma met her face with a backhand, scoring Annabeth's cheek with the osteoderms that had been exposed on the back of her hand at some point during this mission. She yanked the taser she'd gotten back from Ridge out of her waistband and swung her arm up, sending volts of electricity into Annabeth, who swatted the device away. Whether adrenaline or something about her altering, it didn't matter; the device was useless against her.

The scales visible beneath her abraded human skin were iridescent.

Annabeth reached out, grabbing Karma by the shoulder of her shirt, and violently pulled, spinning her around. Her arm, wrapped around Karma's neck, tightened painfully. The muscles undulated, allowing the pressure to continually tighten and cut off her air, despite the strength of Karma's neck muscles.

Tick, tick, tick. Karma threw her weight against the wall, trying unsuccessfully to dislodge Annabeth from her back. Time was running out, and desperation was making her panic. She clawed at the flesh of Annabeth's forearm, revealing more scales.

Semi-familiar with this wing of the hallway, Karma remembered a key box around the corner.

She fought dizziness as she stumbled forward. Her strength and stamina were fading. They'd been fighting off and on for hours. The anxiety of the situation, the fear of getting caught, sapped her energy. Even if she'd been at one hundred percent before entering the building, she'd be struggling now. In her condition now… she couldn't think like that. Lily and Peter would be leaving soon and heading across the fissure. Ridge was out there with Jacob and Allie. And she'd fought too damn hard to get out of here the first time. She'd be damned if she'd spend the last of her life under this roof.

Karma always thought this key box was in a stupid place. It was right around the corner and head height, protruding into the hall. She'd seen too many people walk into it because they were looking at something or someone else and weren't paying attention. The steel box showed no mercy.

Rounding the corner, Karma turned and slammed back into the box. At her height, the back of Annabeth's head slammed into the bottom left edge of the box. Annabeth's grip loosened slightly on impact, and Karma gasped in a lungful of grimy air. Karma repeated the process twice more. A final time, Karma turned her body and spun, slicing Annabeth's arm and back across the sharp edge, opening a long gash that split through her scales, blood pouring from the wound.

The instant Annabeth's weight dropped away, Karma spun and kicked her in the gut, sending her sliding and sprawling down the hallway, leaving a streak of blood in her wake.

Tick, tick, tick. Karma darted into a room across the hall. Lifting a heavy chair from behind the desk, Karma hurled it at the glass window. It splintered and cracked but didn't fall.

Karma growled in frustration and repeated the action.

A spoke on the chair's base pierced the shattered glass and hung in the center of the glass, taunting her. The small but sturdy steel desk mocked her. Using her last burst of adrenaline, Karma heaved the desk up, crying out at the pain radiating over every inch of her body, and launched the desk at the window, at the chair. Both items sailed out the window, and glass rained down.

Karma jumped through, tucking to the side to avoid landing on the desk, which somehow landed upright, with the chair in place, spinning lazily.

The impact of her body on the ground forced another groan from her, but she ignored the pain and shot to her feet, sprinting across the grass, away from the building. A hard shove from behind sent her sprawling, and darkness enveloped her.

Chapter 31

Ridge

Ridge moved quickly through the halls, depositing the explosive contraptions Allie had made. Jacob placed others. Allie carried the supplies.

As he slapped the final one into place, Ridge pushed Allie and Jacob toward an exit door. "Get out and away from the building. I'm going back for Karma."

Allie grabbed his arm, and Jacob stood in front of him. "There's no time. She said she'd meet us out there."

"She's probably already outside, waiting for us," Jacob added.

His frustration bubbled over, and he punched the wall. He should have stayed with her. They never should have separated.

What if Annabeth got the upper hand? What if Karma lost track of time? What if she was too injured to get away?

She wanted to get back to the kids more than anything else. But if something happened to her and Ridge didn't make save himself so *he* could get to the kids, she'd find some way to haunt him, he was sure.

His heart squeezed. He grunted and barreled through the door.

Pale light of the coming day greeted him. They'd been inside all night.

Most of the people fleeing the building from the prior explosions were coated in the same dust and grime as they were. It would be easy to blend in with the crowd and remain undetected. Other Altereds would have as much trouble as he did using their noses. Between the caustic smells left behind by the explosives and the fine particles in the air, unless he were standing over something with an intensely strong scent, he'd never notice.

He scanned the lawn, looking for any hint of Karma.

Jacob and Allie stayed on his heels.

"We need to get further, *now!*" Allie shouted, yanking hard on his arm.

They were almost to the fence line when the concussion of the blast slammed into Ridge's back, throwing him to his knees.

Chaos reigned.

It seemed like slow motion as the first area gave way, caving in on itself and sending more debris into the air. Like dominoes, more areas collapsed, rippling down and around the building, bringing it down piece by piece. The ground rumbled beneath his feet, an echo of the memory of aftershocks, but these were manmade. He'd helped do this.

He needed to find Karma. Hundreds of people crisscrossed the grassy area, screaming in terror. He didn't dare yell Karma's name and alert the Altereds who were in the vicinity, and since his nose was of no use at the moment, he'd only have his eyes to rely on.

He ignored the tugging at his arms by Jacob and Allie. Their strength was no match for him, and he was done with this damn mission. They had the records. They destroyed the facility. They were out. Now, he was going back for Karma, and they would go to the kids.

Ridge laid his hand on a woman's shoulder, and she spun around. Not Karma. A few feet later, another. Not Karma.

"This is going to be like looking for a needle in a haystack. She's not going to stick around here. If she got out—"

Ridge's hand closed over Jacob's throat. "She got out!"

"If she were recognized by someone in the goon squad, she'd be captured in a heartbeat." Allie scratched at his arm, trying to make him let go of Jacob. "Where would she go to get away?"

Ridge loosened his grip. "She got out. She had to." His knees threatened to buckle under him. Panic threatened to choke him. Guilt clawed at his insides. If he made it out, but she didn't... he should have ignored Allie and gone back to where he'd left her, not run from the building with them.

"Ridge, where would she go?"

"She'd go to those kids," Jacob said with his teeth gritted. "Those kids that she mostly hid from the rest of us. Wherever she has them stashed is where she went."

He spun on his heel and went for the fence. He could spend hours here searching for her and never find her. The chaos and sheer number of people made it nearly impossible. In his heart, he knew she'd go to the kids.

They left the lush lawn of Phoenix Corps behind, escaping into the small park Karma often used near the loading docks.

Allie pulled them to a stop at the edge of the trees, pulling Jacob's bag from his back. She pulled out a handful of wires, stuffing them into her pack, and handed the rest to Ridge.

He looked at her quizzically.

"We're leaving here, too," Allie said, taking Jacob's hand. "We aren't built for fighting. We're better at hiding. Take the records with you. Burn them, or keep fighting, that's up to you. I don't know what Malcolm planned to do with them. It's your call now."

Jacob nodded. "Karma once told me about a river to the north. She said there are a couple of places where someone could cross safely."

"Yeah. I took some of the other people from the trailer park there when I helped the rest of you to get out before the goon squad showed up and trashed it." Ridge ripped a thin piece of remaining charred wood from a nearby ruined building and pulled out a mostly blank sheet of paper. There wasn't any groundbreaking information on it, so he turned it over and hastily drew a crude map. "Follow this. You'll be on your own once you cross the water, but this will get you to the safest spot to cross."

"When you see her again..." Jacob said. "Tell her I said thank you for everything."

Ridge held out his hand. Jacob hesitated but reached out and shook it. "Be careful out there."

He closed the backpack and threw it over his shoulder.

He'd head for the kids.

She'd be there. She had to be.

Ridge moved up and down the streets and alleys, ducking into areas he knew he would find a trap or two. He found a half-filled bucket of rainwater and sluiced some over his face to clear the worst of the dirt sticking to him.

Approaching an alley, he noticed the remains of a fire escape crashed into the pavement, and he smiled, remembering that alley. He crossed the street and travelled to an old grocery store. Broken glass still littered the ground around the windows. Toppled shelves dotted the floor, and wires hung drunkenly from the ceiling.

Glass crunched under his boots as he passed through the frame of the once-automatic doors. Registers listed off the edge of the checkout aisles, their drawers dusty and empty, gaping open, likely forced open with tools soon after the first quakes. The retail signs, indicating what had been kept in each aisle, sagged in some places, dangling by one lonely chain in others.

Ridge made his way to the far wall and found the trap he'd come in here for.

The same crunch of glass he heard walking in reached his ears. He spun where he was, putting his back to the wall and squinting his eyes into the darkened shadows of the old store.

Chapter 32

Karma

Someone stepped on her back. She coughed, the action hurting her lungs, back, and ribs. The grit in her eyes burned, and her head pounded. Blades of grass tickled the side of her face, damp from the morning dew. She reached her hand back, the movement slow and creaky. A large lump on the back of her head greeted her. At least her hand came away dry, no blood, she'd probably be just fine. She just needed to get to her feet.

Karma pushed to her hands and knees, the next person who would've stepped on her now tripped over her, their shin colliding with her already abused ribs. She lurched onto her feet to keep from getting more trampled, hunched over, gasping for a good breath of air. The smoke, ash, and dust tasted acrid, and she craved water. She stumbled forward, her throbbing head swiveling back and forth, scanning the lawn for any sign of Ridge, Allie, or Jacob. Everyone running around the property looked the same. A greyish-white dust clung to the hair, clothes, and skin of every person.

As much as she wanted to rid herself of the grime, it would be her best bet to leave it until she was clear of the area.

Karma turned, taking in the sight in front of her now.

Smoke boiled from the fires inside. Large sections of the facility were completely gone, replaced by piles of rubble. Wires swung and sparked between floors.

She turned away from the carnage. Ridge. She needed to find Ridge.

Karma wove through the disoriented people, who were going this way and that. She dodged a few Altereds, but preoccupied with the chaos surrounding them, they didn't pay her any mind. The further away from the wreckage she got, the sparser the people were. She surveyed the area one last time and slipped off the property and into the city. The further away from the compound she moved, the less assault her ears took, and the ringing began to subside.

At the first grimy puddle, Karma scooped the water into her hands. She wasn't desperate enough to drink it, but getting the grit and grime from her face was her top priority. By the time she finished, clouds of dirt swirled in the shallow puddle. Her osteoderms poked through numerous cuts and scrapes along her hands and arms. There were likely just as many spots visible on her face, but at least the coating of sludge that had stuck to her sweaty skin was gone. With it gone, her nose picked up on a few smells. She focused on her favorite: Ridge.

Karma followed his scent to the old, looted grocery store.

Karma crept forward, easing her way through the frame of the door, her shoes crunching on the glass strewn about the floor. Slipping behind a set of toppled shelves, she edged her way further into the large room.

A squeak reached her ears, the sound of rubber soles against the tile floor, a foot adjusting its weight as it prepared to flee or fight.

"Ridge?" She whispered his name, afraid it might not be him, that Phoenix Corps had somehow tricked her.

The screech of metal pierced the thumping of her heart in her ears. In a blur of movement, the shelves in front of her flew, crashing into another set, the cacophony deafening. Her feet left the ground, and the scene around her blurred. One moment, she stood in the middle of the store; the next, the cool concrete wall pressed into her back.

Ridge pressed into her front, breathing hard. His hands roamed her body, checking for injuries, just as she was doing to him.

Karma pulled his head down and pressed her lips to his. Frantic to assure herself he was real, not a mirage, she pulled back, biting her lower lip, inducing pain. He was real. He was here.

A hysterical laugh bubbled up from her chest, and a sob fought for dominance, coming out in a garbled mess. She tugged on his neck, his forehead touching hers. "Didn't I tell you not to steal my traps?" She smiled through the tears pouring down her cheeks. Adrenaline kept her going all night, kept her fighting to get out of there. With Ridge in front of her, it all drained away, leaving her limbs feeling like lead and her body screaming as it registered the pain she was truly in for the first time.

A sly smirk settled over his mouth. "I'll gladly suffer any punishment necessary." He stepped back, but not far enough that he couldn't touch her. His eyes drifted from her head to her toes and back again. "Are you hurt?"

"Tired, sore. Hungry, thirsty. But nothing that I can't live with for a bit. You?"

"There's one thing I can't live without." Ridge's mouth crashed into hers.

They'd made it out alive, relatively unharmed. Heat raced to her core. His weight pinned her to the wall. Delicious warmth seeped into her through the layers of fabric between them. She wanted to bask in his heat, lose herself in his arms.

As it was, she panted, reluctantly pulling her mouth from his. Her knuckles burned from the death grip she had on his shirt, her body unwilling to release him.

His own heaving breaths fluttered the hair around her face. Ridge's hands, wrapped around her lower back, pulling her flush with him, didn't loosen.

"We can't stay here," Karma said it more to herself than to him. "We need to get to the kids."

The frustration in his response was evident. "I know." One of his arms shifted, sliding into her hair, and he pulled her in for one last bruising kiss.

Ridge released her abruptly and stopped away, but clutched her hand in his, lacing their fingers together. He bent and lifted the pack Jacob had been carrying.

Karma looked around. She hadn't seen or smelled Jacob or Allie. "Where...?"

"I told them where and how to cross the river. He said to tell you thank you for everything."

They hurried through the streets, cautious around every corner. The commotion across town at the Phoenix Corps facility brought curious people out of hiding. She scented more people in the streets and guessed that they'd ventured out at the noise, plumes of smoke, and extra debris floating in and around the area. A head or two hid away a split second too late, and she caught momentary glimpses, but otherwise, the streets remained largely abandoned.

Exhaustion dragged at her limbs. She stumbled several times, barely able to lift her boots from the ground. Ridge lifted her into his arms after her next stumble.

"I'm too heavy for you to carry," she protested.

He side-stepped into an alleyway where they'd be hidden from anyone venturing out into the streets, and set her on her feet, keeping his body between hers and the mouth of the alley. "What's wrong?"

"You're as tired as I am. You shouldn't be carrying me."

He caged her in with his body, caressing her cheek with his finger, goosebumps trailing in his wake. Pressing his lips to hers, he deepened the kiss, drawing out a moan. A moan, Karma couldn't be sure whether it came from her or from him.

When he started to pull away, she followed, not wanting it to end. Her heart raced at the simple, yet intense, kiss.

"I like having you in my arms. And I'm not still recovering from some mystery serum that made me sick for months." He cocked his eyebrow at her. "Let me take care of you. You take care of everyone all the time."

"You've done virtually *everything* for the last several months! It's time I—"

He silenced her with another searing kiss. As he gathered her into his embrace, he twisted and lifted her back into his arms, taking her out of the alley and continuing down the street, heading back to where they'd been staying. "No arguing. Rest."

She couldn't help the sigh of contentment and tucked her head into the juncture of his shoulder and neck, inhaling his musky scent. His arms brought her safety, security, and happiness. A smile spread across her face, and her eyes drifted shut, lulled by his warmth and, just... Ridge.

Chapter 33

Ridge

Ridge moved silently through the streets. Her scent surrounded him, and he basked in it. Each scrape and tear in her skin tore at his heart. He needed to remember that she was in his arms and safe, and Phoenix Corps couldn't get to her again. He wouldn't allow it.

He sensed the instant she drifted off to sleep. Her body relaxed a bit more, and she snuggled her nose further into the side of his neck, the warm breath from her exhaled sigh of contentment drifting over his collarbone.

Ridge moved quickly through the streets, hoping to meet the kids before they left. Although if he did catch them before they headed out, they'd be in trouble, because they should have been gone by first light.

When he checked the sky behind him, in the distance, he could make out the dark smoke still rising from the wreckage they had left behind. Out of habit, Ridge took a roundabout way back to the house to hide their scent trail, just in case.

"Put me down, Ridge." Karma's groggy voice reached his ears as she straightened away from him.

"Rest."

"I did. Now put me down."

He obliged, not releasing her until he was sure she was steady on her feet, and even then, he kept his arm around her, tucking her into his side. Her sure-footed steps reassured him that her catnap gave her a boost of energy.

"They should've left by now." There was a distance to her voice, like she didn't realize she spoke out loud.

"They're strong, Karma. They'll be fine until we catch up to them."

She squeezed the fingers she entwined with his. "Thank you," she whispered.

"For what?"

"For everything you've done for me, for them over the last months. I don't rely on others. I've never been able to. I've always had to do it on my own."

Ridged stopped her and gathered her into his arms. "Not anymore. You're stuck with me now. Together, we will navigate the chaos and uncertainty we face."

It was nearing midday when the remainder of the house came into view. Working their way around to the backyard, Ridge felt the emptiness. The kids had done what they asked and did not wait for them to return. The bulkhead door stood open. He led the way down the stairs, his paranoia keeping him alert for the slightest thing out of place.

Once assured the coast was clear, he guided Karma to the couch and tried to sit her down, ignoring her protests. "Rest while I get everything ready to go."

She grabbed the waistband of his jeans and pulled him off balance.

He stumbled, barely catching himself before he knocked them both over.

Karma tugged him behind her and made her way into the bedroom, where their packs still sat on the floor, ready to go. A hard shove from her, and he landed on the bed. "You are right. The kids are tough. We taught them well. If we want to be of *any* help to them when we catch up to them, we *both* need to get a little rest." Karma kicked off her boots and shed the top layer of flannel that survived their ordeal in the facility. A thin t-shirt was all that remained, and he watched in fascination as goosebumps rippled up her arms with the chill of the room.

He shed his own boots and flannel, his jaw cracking with a huge yawn. Scooting up the bed, Ridge held out his arms, encompassing her in his arms, sharing his warmth.

Her voice a sleepy whisper, Karma said, "Sleep a bit. Then we'll eat and get on the road."

Her eyes were heavy again. As the thought registered, his own eyes slammed shut.

Chapter 34

Karma

Heat surrounded her. The scruff of his beard scratched her cheek in the most delicious way. She wanted to purr like a cat, snuggling closer, his arms tightening with her movement.

Reality rushed in. The kids. They needed to get moving.

Waking him with a kiss, she couldn't help the smile forming at his satisfied growl.

"We need to eat and get moving. I want to catch up to them quickly."

Ridge pushed a lock of hair behind her ear. "We'll find them. And we'll find a place to settle. I want more mornings waking up like this." He pulled her in for another lingering kiss, then bounced up and out of bed, dragging her with him, making her laugh.

With a final check of their packs, food in their bellies, and water filling their battered canteens, they left the house behind, closing the bulkhead door behind them—closing off the last bit of their chapter in Fairway.

They kept a steady pace, hiking the length of the fissure until they reached the makeshift bridge.

The kids' scents were muted. They'd been through there hours before. Theirs were the only scents she picked up. The kids were on their own and not followed. The tension she'd held in her shoulders relaxed.

The sun, low in the sky, indicated the lateness of the time. The kids should be finding a place to stop and camp for the night. It would give her and Ridge a chance to catch up.

Once on the other side of the bridge, Karma dropped her pack and approached the edge, looking back at the city she'd known. Too much distance stood between her and Phoenix Corps, but she hoped the faint smoke in the sky was still the smoldering remains of that heinous building.

She heaved her side of the bridge, shoving as hard as she could. The edge gave way on her side of the fissure, and the structure tumbled down the gap, splintering into pieces as it bounced off the sharp rocks and protrusions.

"Feel better now?" Ridge asked, gesturing at the matchsticks now littering the fissure.

"A bit. I'll feel much better when we find the kids." Karma lifted her pack and took Ridge's hand, heading west to follow the kids' path.

They walked through the neighborhood, this side showing even more damage than the other. Charred bits of rubble poked out of piles of ropey, green-leafed vines. The asphalt that used to be the roads in this area was little more than gravel in most places, rolling and crunching beneath their shoes. Large domes of sand, piled high in random areas, remained as evidence of the sand geysers the original quake and its aftershocks caused.

The neighborhood spit them into a field overgrown with weeds, lit up in the growing darkness by thousands of fireflies dancing in the cooling air. They danced out of the way of the pesky humans disturbing their field, twinkling in the shadows of the day.

Under the canopy of the trees, the temperature dropped. Old leaves crunched beneath their feet.

Scurrying sounds reached her ears, and she caught the scent of a few nocturnal animals. She stayed right with Ridge, taking advantage of his better night vision. He'd saved her from several low-hanging branches and raised root systems.

They crossed an old highway, the tall overpass collapsed over the lanes below, its impact leaving a crater filled with hunks of concrete and thick steel beams.

The kids' scents had been getting stronger over the last few hours, driving Karma to pick up her pace. They must be getting closer to them. Faint smoke wafted from somewhere nearby. As they neared the far side of the highway, Karma turned back, the scents getting weaker. She headed toward the crater, Ridge right behind her.

They didn't speak or call out to each other. The further in they climbed, the stronger the scents became.

Karma scurried up a large chunk of concrete, leaning at an angle and propped up by another hunk attached only by bent rebar. Peering over the top, a fire burned down to the last embers, smoldering in the center. Anything else in the small clearing was hidden by other debris. From this angle, a small pathway was visible on the other side. She spun and slid to the ground on her backside, motioning Ridge to follow.

The terrain would have been rugged in daylight, and sharp edges lay in wait for a passing, unsuspecting limb to scrape, but finally the small path she'd spied from above revealed itself.

Heart in her throat, Karma eyed the entrance. Could they have found them?

Ridge laid his hand at the small of her back, comforting and encouraging. "We won't know until we approach. Go ahead. I've got your back." He nodded toward the door, increasing the pressure of his hand on her back.

Drawing in a deep breath, she took the first step forward, then another, and another.

Curled up together for warmth were Lily and Peter. Peter slept peacefully. Lily dozed.

Karma sighed in relief.

At the sound, Lily's eyes sprang open, and a knife appeared in her hand. Recognition lit her face, and she dropped the knife, jumped to her feet, dislodging Peter, and ran to Karma.

Harsh sobs wracked Lily's body, and she clung to Karma. "You're okay! You're back!" Lily repeated over and over between sobs.

Karma rubbed her back, waving at Peter with the other hand as he glued himself to Ridge's side, his eyes still cloudy with sleep, but his beaming smile brought tears to her eyes.

Everyone spoke at once, then burst out laughing.

The laughter. Even though she tried to make sure that the kids had an opportunity to still be kids, they faced so many harsh realities that laughter didn't happen as often as it should have. Karma's laughter released the tears she'd been trying to keep at bay.

"Are you okay?" Peter asked, leaving Ridge's side to lay a gentle hand on Karma's arm.

"Yeah. I'm just so happy to see you guys. It may have only been a little more than a day, but it feels like a lot longer has passed." She lifted her eyes to Ridge, his smile echoing her own.

He stepped forward and wrapped all three of them in a group hug, pressing a kiss on Karma's hair. When he stepped back, he motioned to the area the kids had chosen as their camp. "This was a great choice. There are only a couple of hours left before the sun comes up. Get some more rest. We'll have plenty of time to talk while we travel."

Karma agreed, shooing the kids to their abandoned bedding and curling up beside Ridge near the entrance.

"Rest, too," he whispered in her ear. "I'll keep watch."

"I'm okay. It's your turn."

His heat kept her comfortable while they waited for the sun to rise.

Chapter 35

7619

Ridge

The kids hadn't uttered a single complaint, but even Ridge was getting tired, sore, and cranky. They'd walked for days, weeks now.

One afternoon, they'd had to set up camp earlier than usual because they'd come upon a wide river. Only chest-deep on Karma, the shortest of them, the water temperature was frigid, and it was too close to nightfall to allow them time to dry before the temperatures dropped. Rather than risk hypothermia, they made camp nearby and planned to wait until morning.

A small fire allowed them to cook the morning's catch from their traps and ward off some of the cold from the night, as well as the chilly breeze wafting across the river's surface.

Ridge stood abruptly, staring down the river.

Karma jumped to her feet beside him, her hand on his forearm, the only thing stopping him from taking off. "What is it?"

His palms itched, and he took a step toward the water, away from Karma.

"Ridge?"

His eyes never left the water.

Karma stepped in front of him, but she was too short; he could easily see over her head. The worry radiating off her hit him like a physical blow.

He squeezed his eyes shut, cocking his head, listening. The rushing water drowned out the sounds of anything nearby, but something caught his attention and wouldn't let go.

Karma's cool hands lay against his cheeks, grounding him, drawing his face down to hers.

He dropped his forehead to hers, breathing in her scent, pulling him back. Ridge locked his arms around her, willing his body to stay right there, not follow the pull of a sound he sensed but couldn't hear.

"I don't hear anything, but I hear something calling me." His brow furrowed. "I know it doesn't make sense, but I don't understand it, and I can't explain it."

Karma turned in his arms, her back to his front.

He didn't release her, afraid that if he did, he'd follow whatever it was.

Her chest expanded with her deep inhale. Her sense of smell was a bit better than his. "All I pick up is the water and a few small critters who've been by in the last few hours."

She tried to step away, but he tightened his arms. "Stay." The look she shot him had him rethinking his tone. "Please."

"We can't cross now. It's almost dark." She palmed the knife Lily had when they found the kids. She instructed Lily to put out the fire and prepare the bedrolls. Peter cleaned up. "We're crossing at first light. Stay close and sleep now."

Ridge refused to release Karma, afraid she was the one thing that could keep him from leaving the campsite.

She sat, holding onto his hand, her thumb trailing back and forth over it.

A few minutes later, as quickly as it started, the urge to leave the site disappeared. The tension he held seeped out of his body, leaving him exhausted from the effort.

"Sleep," she told him quietly.

"What if I hear it again?"

"You won't go anywhere. I won't let you." Karma stayed sitting between him and the kids, the knife in her hands and her eyes downriver. "Sleep, Ridge. This time, I've got your back."

His arms wrapped around her leg as he lay next to her. Her fingers, stroking through his hair, lulled him to sleep.

Chapter 36

5713

Karma

The water in the river burned it was so cold. She gritted her teeth and trudged through, keeping a close eye on Ridge and the kids.

Behind her, Lily's teeth chattered.

Ridge kept a hand twisted in Peter's shirt to keep him from being swept downriver with the current.

By the time they reached the other side of the river, the kids collapsed into heaps while Ridge and Karma sucked in air, trying to catch their breath.

In dry clothes as quickly as they could manage, Karma had everyone on their feet and moving away from the banks of the river. She didn't breathe easier until they stopped for the night, after dark, a full day's walk away.

Three days later, the rumble of an engine reached them. Ridge pushed them toward an outcropping of boulders, the only cover in the field. They couldn't see a vehicle or a road, but there was no mistaking that sound.

Ridge held his finger to his lips and motioned for them to wait. Then, he crept away, slinking through the field and out of her sight.

This was the first time they had evidence of people since leaving Fairway.

Minutes passed. Karma worried her hands together.

"He'll be back," Peter assured her confidently.

Karma smiled. "I know."

"The waiting is hard, I know," he said, sounding much too grown-up for his age.

She chucked Peter on the chin. These kids amazed her at every turn.

Her patience at its end, she stood, getting ready to follow Ridge, in case he'd run into trouble, when he came back into view. She directed the kids to stay where they were and raced to his side.

"There's a huge city not far from here. People everywhere," he said when she caught up to him.

Relief and panic warred within her for top billing. A lot of people could mean safety, blending into the crowd. A lot of people could increase the danger, more eyes to spy and alert someone that they didn't belong.

Panic must have been the emotion written on her face because Ridge took her hand and pulled her close. "I'll keep you safe. All of you."

She pressed her lips to his. "I know you will."

The buildings in town towered over them as they entered the city.

Karma knew she looked haggard, if the way the others looked was any indication. They kept their heads down and moved through the crowds, keeping to the edges to have at least one avenue of escape.

Most of the people walking around wore opulent clothes, at least opulent to the standards she was used to. She was poor before the quake.

Bright colors and elaborate shapes sauntered down the streets. Fancy cars whizzed by in a blur.

Peter held her hand, squeezing it tight in terror and awe. Lily made herself as small as possible, huddling near Ridge.

The smells of spices, vegetables, and meat she hadn't had in a decade made her mouth water and her stomach growl loudly.

They wandered past the large window of a store with televisions of all sizes, all tuned to the same channel. A KQKE news report banner scrolled across the bottom of the screen while a female reporter with dark hair and eyes gave an account of the local and national news. The sound was muffled, but the map behind her had a pin labeled Fairway, and pictures flipping next to her with images of rubble, what was left of the Phoenix Corps building.

She grabbed Ridge's hand, needing the physical connection with him. Karma couldn't tear her eyes from the images on the screen.

A minute later, the images blinked away as the reporter moved onto another story, breaking the spell that held Karma in place.

She twisted to face Ridge. News was getting out of Fairway, obviously. She hadn't seen their faces on the news report, but could they have been shown earlier? Were people looking for them? What if they were? What would happen to the kids? Maybe they shouldn't have come to a city. Maybe they should have stayed in the wilderness they'd just traversed. They could have trapped food, built shelter. They could have made it work.

Ridge's fingers were on her chin, tilting her face up to his."

Stay with me, Karma. Whatever has you panicked, we'll deal with it together. Deep breaths."

Lily tugged at her sleeve. "We'll draw less attention over there." She pointed to a small alcove between shops a couple of dozen yards away.

The four of them moved into the alcove, Karma pushing the kids in behind her, prepared to defend them against anything that came near. Ridge stayed closest to the sidewalk and street.

She found herself matching his breathing as he stared into her eyes and pulled in deep, slow breaths.

"Do you want to leave? We can leave now and never return."

Karma glanced back at the kids. Winter was coming. It would be too cold for them before she could build a shelter, even with Ridge's help.

He nodded, agreeing with the concerns she voiced.

"I don't even know where to go from here! We don't have money, and we don't know who we can trust. What have we done?"

"You kept us safe. You kept us together," Lily said. "We'll figure it out."

"Yeah," Peter piped in.

"Let's walk around a bit more. See what we can see, okay? Then we'll make a decision based on that." Ridge held his hand out to her. Between the chilly temperature and her fear, it felt hot compared to the icy chill in hers.

A couple of blocks away, the noise of the street grew exponentially. Shouting and laughter could be heard before they reached the corner.

Colorful tapestries hung from wooden stalls lining both sides of the street. Vendors shouted into the crowd, trying to draw people to their booths. The mouthwatering scents permeated the air as steam rose from makeshift stoves, fires, and grills. Even above the cacophony, the sound of the kids' growling stomachs reached her ears. As much as she didn't want to enter the crowd, feeling claustrophobic even thinking about it, she would have the best chance of getting food for the kids here.

The blur of colors as the crowd undulated down the street hypnotized her. She couldn't tear her eyes away.

They merged with the crowd, moving along down the street. A few vendors called out, offering free samples to grab the attention of possible customers. Ridge urged her forward.

The bite was hot, the spices exploding in her mouth, warming her from the inside out. The strange man at the stove stared at her, his golden amber eyes boring through her. His flame-red hair with random streaks of platinum blonde caught her attention. He was taller than Ridge by at least a couple of inches.

Ridge's arm came around her, his hand splaying across her belly, holding her tight to him. He gripped her shirt in his fist and pulled, trying to maneuver her behind him, but she held fast.

A woman with dark hair pulled into a tight bun walked up behind the man, placing her hand at the small of his back. She too stared at Karma. Her eyes flicked to Ridge, then the kids, and back to her. She patted the man's back and stepped around him. His lips thinned in response.

She held out two bowls of thick soup, each with a hunk of crusty bread on top, and nodded to the kids. "For the children." With her arm outstretched, the sleeve of her shirt rode up. At the very bottom of the sleeve, Karma could make out the bottom of a "C," a replica of the one on her forearm, but done in black ink, not the shimmery iridescent ink of hers. The woman's tattoo was also missing the identification numbers.

Karma dragged her eyes from the tattoo and looked at the woman, who met her with an unwavering gaze.

"Take it," she urged. "There's no agenda. No child should be left hungry."

Cautiously, Karma took the bowls, handing one to each of the kids.

The woman scooped two more bowls for her and Ridge. "Are you new to the city?"

Ridge responded to the tension ratcheting higher in her body, tightening his arm around her.

When the woman reached forward, Karma's hand shot out, taking hold of the woman's wrist and pushing her sleeve up higher.

The man reacted, vaulting over the counter at the front of their booth.

An icy chill raced over Karma, and her knees buckled with the pain, like thousands of ice shards penetrating all over her body.

Ridge pulled Karma behind him, dislodging the man's arm and grabbing him by the throat.

Ice crystals formed on Ridge's hand and wrist.

Before Karma could shake off the pain and intervene, the woman reached forward and laid her hand on the man's forearm. His grip relaxed, and he released Ridge, who cradled his frost-covered arm against his stomach and stepped back, but kept himself between the two strangers and the kids.

Everything happened in the blink of an eye. The kids stood frozen, their mouths agape at the scene before them.

The woman pivoted, keeping the man behind her, and lifted her sleeve. "You reacted to my tattoo. I assume you are familiar with them?"

"You could say that."

"Your hair doesn't quite cover your neck. Your scales are peeking through when the wind blows."

Karma's hand shot to her neck to cover the translucent skin. It hadn't been long enough for the largest of the gashes she received to heal over and have the skin become opaque again.

"Have you left the facility recently?" she asked.

Karma didn't answer.

The violence of moments ago seemingly forgotten, she nodded. "Understandable that you don't want to share that information with me. There's a shelter a few blocks from here. They help newcomers to the city to find work and housing." The woman reached behind her and grabbed a ripped piece of paper, scribbling down an address and handing it to her. "They won't ask questions, and they won't search you. Most everyone stays to themselves. So, the kids will be safe there, too. We've not been here long ourselves. You may see us there. Rest assured, we will keep your secret. We appreciate the same courtesy." After a bit of a pause, she added, "You probably don't trust me, and I don't blame you. But you will find warm beds to sleep in and assistance." She scanned the market before lowering her voice. "Even if it wouldn't be too cold for the kids to sleep outside, you don't want to be caught by the government officials with nowhere to go. They tend to *find* places to send the homeless."

Not sure what to do or say, Karma gave a single nod of her head and took a step back, bringing Ridge with her.

The woman held up the bowls, abandoned when the man leapt over the counter. "Please. Take them. Eat. Then find safety for your young ones."

Chapter 37

Karma

Karma led the kids away from the market, into a quieter street, and they moved to a bench set off to the side to sit and eat their soup. She was hesitant to take the help, and if it were just her, she wouldn't. But the kids needed to eat something, and this would be the freshest and most nutritious meal they'd had in a long time. It smelled and tasted delicious.

She stepped away from the kids, pulling Ridge with her. "What is your opinion on going to this place?" she asked, holding up the slip of paper with hastily jotted down directions and a barely legible address.

"I think that we don't have a lot of options right now. I'll keep you safe. I'll keep the kids safe."

Closing the distance, Karma wrapped her arms around him. "We'll keep each other safe."

Soon after practically licking the bowls clean, they disposed of their trash and started down the street, following the directions from the woman in the market.

The section of the city they entered appeared rougher than the area with the market. People wandered the streets with duller, less lavish clothes and kept their heads down as they moved around. The older buildings had a dingy quality, not nearly as well-maintained as the section they entered. It reminded her of her section of Fairway before the quake, a poor neighborhood, but safe from the tagging and drugs in the other, more dangerous, areas of the city.

Several streets further, they came to a tall, red brick building with large, steel double doors. The sidewalks around the building were clear of trash, and cheerful light emanated from the windows on the upper floors as the day's shadows grew longer.

Taking a steadying breath, Karma stepped up to the door and knocked. If she was going to take the risk of bringing the kids here, she would take the lead and take responsibility for any consequences that might result from this.

The bong of the steel echoed into the room beyond.

"Someone is coming," Ridge said.

A few seconds later, the footsteps were close enough for her to hear them, too.

The door swung open, and a petite woman stood inside, a mountain of a man behind her. Ridge might've heard her steps, but the ones Karma heard belonged to him.

"Can I help you?" Her voice reminded Karma of Rosie.

"A woman from the market sent us in this direction. We are new to the city and don't have anywhere to go yet."

"The market? Oh, I know who sent you. Come on in out of the cold." She retreated from the entrance, the mountain of a man staying right behind her. "I'm Clara. This is Harmony House." She beckoned them inside with a sweep of her arm. Catching sight of the kids, she smiled warmly. "A whole family! We don't have a lot of space, but if you don't mind sharing, we have a room with four cots available with a shared bathroom just a few steps down the hall."

"That would be ideal. Thank you."

"We will help you to get on your feet, find a job, and keep your bellies full. Everyone pitches in around here. Expectations are that, until you find a job, you will help and pull a little extra weight around here, to lighten the load of those who have found work."

"Of course."

"Do you have any particular skills?"

"I'm fairly handy at repairing things," Karma said.

Clara's eyes lit up. "That could be very helpful indeed!"

"I can learn. I'm a fair hand at cooking, though," Ridge added.

"Since our main cooks, whom you met, are at the market most days, your help in the kitchen will be an asset." The mountain of a man had the voice of a ten-pack-a-day smoker, deep and gravelly.

"Gerald here, he's been working his hands to the bone in the kitchen since they went to the market. He'll definitely appreciate the help."

"The kids can shadow me," Karma added before another suggestion could be made. "They've been learning alongside me for a while now. They've learned a lot."

"Of course, dear." Clara's smile was sincere. "Bring your bags and follow me."

Clara led them up three flights of stairs and down the hall, a few doors to the only open doorway. "There are fresh sheets on each of the beds and lockers in the corner for all of your belongings. Settle in, and then you can come down for a meal."

"We ate at the market. If you don't mind, I think we may just turn in for the night."

"Absolutely. Come down when you wake up tomorrow morning, and we will show you around. Show you where you can help." Clara closed the door behind her after wishing them a good night.

Karma threw the bolt lock across the moment Clara was out of earshot, her back against the door.

Unremarkable slate gray walls lined the room, and four utilitarian cots, like the ones she'd scavenged, took up the majority of space in the room.

Lily and Peter set their packs down and started making their beds.

Ridge approached her, pulling her pack off and leaving it next to his on the floor. "We'll be careful. We'll be watchful. But this is the best-case scenario for us."

"What about the files?" Her eyes drifted to the pack containing them, then back to him.

Ridge studied her face. "What do you want to do with them?"

"I think we hold onto them until we know a bit more about this place. There are too many unknowns, and we can't risk endangering the kids or losing the leverage these files could provide until we know more."

Karma stepped into Ridge's embrace and held on. She lifted her chin and reached up, pulling him down until his lips met hers.

"We are safe, warm, fed, and together. Whatever is next for us, we handle it together."

"Together," he echoed.

THE END

Thank you for reading! While this is the end of Karma and Ridge for a bit, don't worry, we'll see them again. But first, we need to meet some of their new friends and find out about the other places affected by these disasters and what Phoenix Corps has been doing there! Next up, is Fate and the area devastated by a super volcano.

Did you miss Breaking Point, the prequel that reports on the disasters as they happen? Head to
https://dl.bookfunnel.com/3a6i8jyj0d
to claim your copy of the prequel

Speaking of Breaking Point, do you want to get a peek into Cassandra and Bryce? Find out where they are now? There is an exclusive scene at the end of each duology where you get to see Cassandra and Bryce reporting the events at the end of each book 2. To get your copy of the scene following Karma's Here, go to https://dl.bookfunnel.com/m9a0q9todr.

Acknowledgements

First, thank you to all of you who have read this book through to the end. Thank you for coming along on this journey with me! I truly hope you enjoyed it. Hopefully there will be many more adventures together in our futures!

This book would have never been possible without the support of my amazing husband and beautiful daughters. I can never thank them enough.

To my Yas, I cannot express how much your support and cheerleading helped to get me through the imposter syndrome moments. And a special thank you to the QueenYa for all of your help in 'fixing' my attempts to create a cover, logo, bookmark, etc. and advice on my small business! As always, the covers shine after being in your masterful hands!

To my Author Ever After community, thank you for lighting the fire under me and helping to walk me through the intimidating process of self-publishing. To my WWF crew, thank you for keeping me on task... sometimes, and holding me accountable for getting words and making posts.

Also by Jillian Beane

<u>Altered Karma Series</u>

Karma's Coming (Jan 2026)

Karma's Here (Feb 2026)

Fate's Stories (2 books) *Publish Dates TBA*

Destiny's Stories (2 books) *Publish Dates TBA*

Series wrap up – *Publish Dates TBA*

About Jillian

Jillian has been writing since high school. Finally published 25+ years later, she has had oodles of careers to keep her busy along the way....

Stay-at-home mom

Preschool Teaching Assistant

Licensed Journeyman Plumber

Secret Squirrel

Security for a Professional Baseball Team

Disability Adjudicator

Credit Card Fraud Investigator

Does she know what she wants to do when she grows up? Nah! Where's the surprise in that?!?!

Surrounded by the support of her loving husband, her two amazing and crazy kids, and her family, she is adding AUTHOR to her ever-growing list of careers.

When she isn't writing action packed fantasy adventures full of found family and love, you can find her reading, watching movies, listening to music, or hanging out with her Yas at their favorite art studio getting into ALL the shenanigans. Whether creating with her words or her hands, Jillian finds joy in art of all forms, be it remodeling or building projects, crochet, painting on canvas or pottery, or simply sitting in front of the dreaded blinking cursor, preparing to go on an adventure with her imaginary friends.

www.ingramcontent.com/pod-product-compliance
Lightning Source LLC
Chambersburg PA
CBHW020126310726

48970CB00006B/1738